**From the desk of Emerald Larson,
owner and CEO of Emerald, Inc.**

To: My personal assistant, Luther Freemont

Re: My grandson Lucien Garnier

Lucien is in the process of incorporating
Laurel Enterprises into his own company,
Garnier Construction. But it's recently been
brought to my attention that he's entertaining the
idea of having an heir of his own to inherit his
holdings when the time comes for him to retire.
I've been told by a very reliable source that he's
asked his executive assistant, Haley Rollins, to
help him with this project and she's agreed.

If my source is correct—and I have no reason
to believe otherwise—Lucien is going to need a
push in the right direction if this is to come to a
satisfactory conclusion. I expect you to arrange
whatever you deem necessary to accomplish that
goal.

As always, I am relying on your complete
discretion in this matter.

Emerald Larson

Dear Reader,

For those of you who have read the first three
THE ILLEGITIMATE HEIRS books, I'm happy to tell
you that Emerald Larson is at it again. She's found three
more of her grown grandchildren and she's determined to
see they find happiness with their soul mates, as well as
take their rightful place within her empire. And if this is
your first experience reading about Emerald, Inc. and the
recently discovered grandchildren of one of the richest,
most powerful women in the corporate world, you're in for
a real treat.

In *Bossman Billionaire,* Emerald's grandson Luke Garnier
decides to hire a surrogate to help him produce an heir to
inherit his holdings when the time comes for him to retire.
But when he finds that the surrogacy laws in his state
prevent him from proceeding as planned, he turns to his
attractive executive assistant, Haley Rollins, to help him
get what he wants.

I'm in no way an expert on surrogacy laws and, because
laws change from time to time, I've blended fact, fiction
and creative license to create a story that I hope will be
with you long after you finish the book. So please, sit back
and enjoy the latest installment of Emerald Larson and her
ILLEGITIMATE HEIRS.

All the best,

Kathie DeNosky

KATHIE DeNOSKY

BOSSMAN BILLIONAIRE

Published by Silhouette Books

America's Publisher of Contemporary Romance

 SILHOUETTE BOOKS

Recycling programs
for this product may
not exist in your area.

ISBN-13: 978-0-373-76957-5

BOSSMAN BILLIONAIRE

Copyright © 2009 by Kathie DeNosky

Visit Silhouette Books at www.eHarlequin.com

Printed in U.S.A.

KATHIE DeNOSKY

lives in her native southern Illinois with her big, lovable Bernese mountain dog, Nemo. Highly sensual stories with a generous amount of humor, Kathie's books have appeared on the Waldenbooks bestseller list and received a Write Touch Readers' Award and a National Readers' Choice Award. She enjoys going to rodeos, traveling to research settings for her books and listening to country music. Readers may contact Kathie at P.O. Box 2064, Herrin, Illinois 62948-5264 or e-mail her at kathie@kathiedenosky.com. They can also visit her Web site at www.kathiedenosky.com.

This series is dedicated to Charlie, the love of my life.

A special thank you to Kristi Gold and Roxann Delaney
for laughing with me, crying with me and being there
for me through the ups and downs.
I couldn't ask for better friends. You're the best.

And to Tina Colombo for believing in me
through thick and thin. I can't thank you enough.

Prologue

"We're not for sale, Mrs. Larson," Lucien Garnier refused flatly. "And I'm sure you'll agree that trying to build a relationship of any kind at this stage is out of the question."

Completely unaffected by his blunt statement, Emerald Larson stared across her highly polished Louis XIV desk at one of her recently discovered grown grandchildren. She could understand his and his two siblings' anger. It had to have been quite disconcerting to discover that instead of the struggling artist he'd portrayed himself to be, their father Neil Owens was really Owen Larson, the philandering, footloose offspring of one of the richest, most powerful women in the corporate world. But then, she hadn't been overly happy to learn that in his youth, her late son had left a bevy of women pregnant and on their own.

Since learning of her grandchildren, Emerald had arranged for all of Owen's children to claim their birthright and take their rightful place within the Emerald, Inc. corporate empire. She had successfully built a relationship with her three other grandsons and set them up with companies of their own, but the trouble was, she didn't know exactly how many children Owen had fathered or even if she'd found all of them. It was only in the past few months she'd learned that her son had impregnated yet another woman—not once, but twice. His affair with a young Frenchwoman visiting the San Francisco area on a student visa had resulted in a set of twin sons, Lucien and Jacques. Then, ten years later, Owen had returned to the woman and rekindled the affair, only to leave the poor dear girl pregnant again, this time with a daughter, Arielle.

The fact that Francesca Garnier had been the only woman Owen had returned to was bittersweet for Emerald. It was heartening to learn that her hedonistic son had loved the woman as much as he was capable of loving anyone, but disappointing to realize that in the end, his self-absorption had won out and he'd left Francesca behind—just as he'd done with the others.

But the past was just that—the past. There was little Emerald could do about what had taken place all those years ago. The only thing to be done now was to forge ahead and focus her efforts on righting things between herself and the three Garnier siblings.

"I can well understand your irritation, Lucien, but think about what I'm offering you and your brother and sister. Each of you will receive a multimillion-dollar trust fund, as well as complete control of one of my companies."

"We don't need your money or your company," Jacques reiterated.

"I understand that you and Lucien are wealthy enough in your own right now to never want for anything," Emerald acknowledged, nodding. Turning her attention to her only granddaughter, she smiled. "But what about you, darling? I'm sure your teaching salary is adequate enough to provide you with the basics, but what I'm offering is financial security for the rest of your life. You'll never have to worry about taking care of yourself or your—"

"Arielle is fine," Lucien interrupted, his glare formidable. "Jake and I have always taken care of our sister and we always will. We'll see that she has everything she needs."

"And you should both be commended for the sacrifices you've made to raise her." Emerald was completely impervious to his dark expression. "After your mother's untimely death, you not only did an excellent job of taking care of your sister, you both held jobs, as well as finished your education. That's a huge undertaking for two boys barely twenty years old."

"We wouldn't have thought to do it any other way," Lucien countered, shrugging off her compliment.

Emerald watched the girl eye one brother and then the other before Arielle sat forward in her chair.

"I could never express how much I appreciate everything the two of you have done for me throughout the years," Arielle spoke up, finally breaking her silence.

"But I'm a grown woman now, Luke, and I'm perfectly capable of taking care of myself and making my own decisions." She turned her full attention on Emerald. "Luke and Jake might not be interested in what you're offering, Mrs. Larson, but I certainly am."

"No, you're not." The twin brothers glared daggers at their younger sister.

"Oh, yes, I am."

Arielle's determination was almost palpable and it did Emerald's heart good to see that her granddaughter didn't seem the least bit affected by her older brothers' intimidating scowls. The child reminded Emerald of herself some fifty years ago.

"You two can do what you please, but I'm going to accept the trust fund and whatever company Mrs. Larson deems suitable for me to take over."

Their lack of agreement on the issue was the very opening Emerald had been looking for to seal the deal. "If you'll excuse me for a few moments, I have something that requires my immediate attention," she interjected, rising from her desk chair. "While I'm gone, I think it would be wise for the three of you to discuss my proposal." Walking to the door, she turned back. "But keep in mind, this is all or nothing. You all agree to accept everything or forfeit the opportunity completely."

Stepping into the outer office, she pulled the door shut behind her and walked over to her assistant's desk. "Get the acceptance papers ready for my grandchildren to sign, Luther."

"Have they accepted your gift, madam?" Luther Freemont asked in his usually stiff manner as he reached for a file on his desk.

Emerald glanced at her closed office door, smiling contentedly. "Not yet. But rest assured, they will."

She hadn't intended to put stipulations on her gift to the Garnier siblings, but her twin grandsons' determination to decline her generosity left her little choice. Being one of a few women over the past fifty years to carve out her place in the "good old boy" network of the corporate world, she'd learned when and how to manipulate a situation to her benefit. And she certainly wasn't above pulling out all the stops to get what she wanted—even if that meant playing hardball with her own grandchildren.

Confident that everything was going her way, Emerald glanced at the clock on Luther's desk. The Garnier siblings should have had ample time to reach an agreement.

"I'll page you when we're ready to sign the documents, Luther," she instructed, walking back to the door.

When she re-entered her private office, she smiled at her grandchildren still seated in front of her desk. It was time to incorporate the Garnier siblings into the Emerald, Inc. empire.

One

"Haley, I want my calendar cleared for the day and you to be in my office in five minutes. There's something I need you to do."

Haley Rollins stared open mouthed as Lucien, or as he preferred to be called, Luke Garnier passed her desk on the way into his private office. For the past five years, every weekday morning at promptly eight-thirty, he'd arrived at the corporate offices of Garnier Construction, ordered her to get him coffee and expected her to be in his office to review his day's itinerary. But today he was more than half an hour early and failed even to mention the requisite cup of coffee.

What on earth could have happened that would cause a man so set in his ways to deviate from his routine?

Something was definitely in the works and if the

look on his handsome face was any indication, he considered it to be of the utmost importance. Her usual Monday morning slump vanished.

Reaching for her phone, Haley made quick work of rescheduling his appointments, then after a quick trip to the break room for the coffee she knew he wanted, entered Luke's office a few minutes later. But as she walked across the room, her eyes widened and she had to remind herself to breathe. She never got tired of looking at the sexiest man she'd ever seen.

He had removed his suit coat and stood at the plate glass window behind his desk, staring pensively at the downtown Nashville traffic on the busy street below. With his hands stuffed into the front pockets of his trousers, the gray fabric had pulled taut over his tightly muscled derriere, drawing her attention to the narrowness of his hips, while at the same time his crisply pressed, tailored white shirt emphasized the width of his broad shoulders. The contrast was amazing and a testament to his excellent physical condition. And it was becoming increasingly difficult to hide her reaction to him.

"You're three minutes late," he said without turning around.

Bringing her wayward thoughts in check, she calmly set his coffee mug on the desk. "I had several calls to make in order to free up your day."

She wasn't surprised that he knew the moment she walked into the room, even though the plush carpet made the sound of her late entrance inaudible. Luke Garnier missed very little. And he never hesitated to comment on his observations. Ever.

"Sit down, Haley. There's something I want to talk over with you." His tone of voice denoted the serious nature of their discussion and for the briefest of moments, a tiny shiver of trepidation coursed through her.

She'd been extremely careful, but had he finally realized that his efficient, reliable, emotionless executive assistant had done the unthinkable? Had he discovered that she'd developed a huge crush on him practically from the moment he interviewed her for the job five years ago? That she might even be in love with him?

Seating herself in the leather armchair in front of his desk, she gave herself a mental shake. Her feelings for him had been the only thing that he'd failed to detect and she had no reason to believe that had changed. She'd never given him the slightest indication that she viewed him as anything more than her workaholic boss. A boss who made no secret of the fact that he had no interest in anything that took his attention away from Garnier Construction. His business was a very demanding mistress and that was just the way he preferred it.

"How was your trip to Wichita this weekend?" she asked when he continued to stare out the window. He hadn't shared the reason for his last-minute trip or whom he'd been meeting with, but Haley had no doubt it was the cause of his early arrival at the office this morning. "Did everything go well?"

His shoulders slowly rose and fell, indicating he took a deep breath before he finally turned to face her. "It actually depends on how you look at the outcome."

His noncommittal answer confused her. She'd never known Luke Garnier to be indecisive about anything.

He was the type of man who viewed things as either black or white, up or down, right or wrong. Gray areas in his business or his personal life were quite simply nonexistent.

Frowning, Haley shook her head. "I'm not sure I understand."

"I wouldn't expect you to." His intense blue gaze pinned her to the chair for several long moments as he decided exactly how much he wanted her to know about the meeting, then raking his hand through his thick black hair, he took another deep breath. "I've just become the new owner of Laurel Enterprises."

She couldn't have stopped her surprised gasp if she'd tried. "This is huge, Luke. Laurel Enterprises is the largest, most successful builder of vacation rentals and log homes in eastern Tennessee. Maybe in the entire state."

He nodded. "Laurel and all of its holdings are mine now."

"Congratulations! How on earth did you get Emerald, Inc. to relinquish it?" she asked, somewhat in awe of the achievement. She had seen him accomplish several seemingly impossible goals in the past, but obtaining Laurel Enterprises from the infamous Emerald Larson had to be an all-time best, both professionally and personally.

"Let's just say I had the inside track on gaining control of Laurel and leave it at that for now," he replied, giving her a one-shouldered shrug.

His answer only served to confuse her even further. As his executive assistant, Haley knew almost as much about Luke's vision and goals for Garnier Construction as he did. And she couldn't, for the life of her, figure out why he wasn't more triumphant about the acquisition. For someone whose already quite lucrative construction company had just doubled in size, he was being extremely reserved about it.

But she knew better than to ask why he wasn't more enthused. If he wanted her to know how he'd pulled off the deal, he would tell her.

"Well, whatever magic you used to convince them to sell to you worked beautifully. You've been wanting to expand into that area of the business for some time." She smiled. "Shall I set up an appointment with your attorney to examine the purchase agreement?"

"No, all paperwork was taken care of over the weekend."

"Should I contact your banker to have the funds transferred?"

"No need. Laurel has already been signed over to me. *Free* and clear."

Surely she'd misunderstood. "Excuse me? Did you say *free?*"

When his vivid blue eyes met hers, he gave her a half smile. "Yes."

Unable to believe what she was hearing, Haley sat forward. "Emerald Larson, the most successful woman in the corporate world, the first woman to crack the top five of the Fortune 500 list, just *gave* you the company?"

"Yes, but that's not what I want to discuss with you," he said, his tone indicating that the subject was closed. He lowered himself into the high-backed executive chair behind his desk. "I've come to the realization that now that I own the largest construction company in the

South, I need someone to ensure the continuance of Garnier Construction long after I'm gone. I need an heir."

She wasn't sure what shocked her more, his admission that Emerald Larson had handed him Laurel Enterprises on a silver platter or that he suddenly thought he needed someone to inherit his assets. "What brought this on?" she blurted before she could stop herself.

To her surprise, he didn't seem at all upset that she was questioning his decision. "My brother and sister aren't the least bit interested in the construction business," he explained. "Jake is perfectly content being the most expensive divorce lawyer in Tinseltown and Arielle adores teaching preschool kids whatever children that age need to learn. That's why I've decided to hire a surrogate and produce an heir of my own."

Haley knew her expression conveyed her disbelief, but she was beyond caring. "Don't you think that's a little drastic? Having a child is a huge step."

Luke shook his head. "It makes perfect sense. To make sure that the Garnier name will be a force to reckon with in the construction business for decades to come."

"And you think that having a child will make that happen?"

"I believe it tips the odds in my favor, yes."

"But it will take years before a child would be ready to learn all that you have to teach."

"That's why the sooner I get started, the better."

Luke could tell from the look in her turquoise eyes that Haley thought he'd lost his mind. And truth to tell, he wasn't entirely sure he hadn't done that very thing.

But after seeing Emerald Larson's desperation to

find family members to take over her vast holdings, he'd realized that building a corporate empire meant nothing without someone to carry on the legacy. That's why he had thought about who would take over his company and what they would do with it when the time came for him to retire.

It had taken a couple of sleepless nights, but to be certain Garnier Construction continued to grow and prosper long after he was gone, he concluded he would have to spend years grooming his own replacement. And who would have more of a vested interest in learning all that he knew than his own son?

That's when he'd decided to have a child. Luke could start by taking him to the job sites as a toddler, then by the time the boy understood how to avoid the pitfalls of the business and how to encourage Garnier's growth, he'd already be familiar with the way the operation worked.

"Are you really serious about hiring someone to have your baby?" she asked, finally finding her voice.

"Yes."

He wasn't at all surprised by Haley's astonishment. He'd had much the same disbelieving reaction himself when the idea first took shape. But the more he'd thought about it, the more it made sense to hire a surrogate from a reputable agency in order to produce his heir. The last thing he wanted or needed was the hassle of finding someone, then the trouble of convincing the woman to have his child without the slightest possibility of a future together. It would be much easier to choose a woman who had already decided to serve as a surrogate.

"If you think about it, it's actually the smart thing to do."

She raised one light brown eyebrow. "Maybe it makes sense to you. But I seem to be missing your rationale on this."

Why he felt compelled to explain himself to her was something of a mystery. He never explained his reasoning or actions to anyone, for anything. But he suddenly felt it was very important that Haley understand.

"I need an heir. I don't have a wife, nor do I want one. That's why surrogacy is the obvious answer. I get what I want without any further obligation to the boy's mother. Once the heir is born, she goes her way and I take the child and go mine."

"And you're definitely going through with this?" she asked, looking more doubtful with each passing second.

"Yes." He leaned back in his desk chair. "I want you to research the state laws and compile a list of reputable agencies specializing in surrogacy. I'll expect it on my desk by noon."

"Is there anything else you need?" she inquired, rising to leave.

"No. That will be all for now."

As he watched her close the door to his office, Luke could tell that she strongly disapproved of his decision. But he knew her well enough that she wouldn't voice her objections. And that was one of the many reasons Haley Rollins made the perfect executive assistant. She was amazingly efficient, had business instincts that rivaled his own and knew when to voice her opinions and when to keep them to herself.

An hour later, Haley breathed a tiny sigh of relief as she closed the Internet browser on her computer. It appeared that Luke would have to forego his plan of producing an heir through a surrogate. From everything she found on the subject, the state of Tennessee had taken a clear stand and only allowed married couples to enter into surrogacy agreements.

Nibbling on her lower lip, she glanced at his closed office door. It wasn't that she didn't think Luke should have a child of his own. She did. But only for the right reasons. And she certainly didn't consider having a baby simply because he needed someone to run Garnier Construction eventually to be one of them.

Unfortunately, her boss wasn't the type to give up that easily. He'd made up his mind, set his course of action and that was that. There wasn't a doubt in her mind that he would somehow find a way to get what he wanted. He always did.

Her chest tightened at the thought. She'd been giving babies a lot of thought herself after receiving a birth announcement from a friend and would give almost anything to have a baby. Considering her feelings for Luke, she'd like nothing more than for him to be her baby's daddy. But aside from the fact that he'd never looked at her as anything more than his extremely competent executive assistant, she wanted all the things he wanted to avoid. She wanted love, marriage and the close family life she'd never had.

She slowly pushed away from her desk and walked over to tap on his office door. There was no sense in thinking about any of that now. His plan had run into a huge obstacle and was effectively stalled, at least for the time being.

"Luke?" He was on the phone and motioned for her

to enter, so she seated herself in front of his desk as she waited for him to end the conversation.

"I'll be there on Saturday. Set up a special meeting for me with the office staff, then I want to visit the job sites to meet the construction crews. In the meantime, reassure them that I have no plans to make any major changes. Their jobs are just as secure now as they were when Emerald, Inc. owned Laurel Enterprises."

Hanging up the phone, he turned his attention her way. "I take it that you've already compiled the list of surrogacy agencies?"

"I didn't get that far," she stated, shaking her head. "It appears that your plan has run into a bit of a snag."

"And that would be?" he prompted.

"State law allows only married couples to hire surrogates."

She could tell when he rubbed the back of his neck with his hand that he wasn't at all happy with the news. "Are there any exceptions?"

"If there are, I couldn't find them." Shrugging, she added, "There are a few states where the law is more liberal on surrogacy, but this isn't one of them. However, it doesn't appear to be illegal to enter into a verbal agreement with a woman as long as there's no compensation other than medical expenses and she willingly signs over her rights to the child."

"Did you consult with my attorney?" he asked, a deep frown creasing his forehead.

She shook her head. "Mr. Clayton is out of town for the next week and I hesitated calling anyone else due to the discretion needed for a matter this sensitive. Besides, from everything I could find on the issue, the state law is quite consistent—married couples only."

Luke nodded slowly but remained silent, mentally reviewing what new course of action to take. "In other words, I need to find a woman with the traits I want and one who would also sign over her custodial rights immediately after giving birth." He looked thoughtful for several long moments. "That would be taking a huge risk without the protection of a binding contract."

Haley should have known he'd immediately start thinking of other options to obtain his goal. That was the way Luke worked. When he ran into a roadblock, he found the best way around it.

But the thought of another woman bearing his child caused a tight knot to form in the pit of her stomach and she suddenly felt the need to escape his presence. "I've decided to take the rest of the day off," she announced, quickly rising to her feet. "And if I were you, I wouldn't count on me being here tomorrow."

"Why? What's wrong?"

She wasn't surprised by his puzzled expression. In the five years she'd worked for him, she had never taken time off other than her annual two-week vacation. But she wasn't about to explain what she didn't fully understand herself. He wouldn't want to hear her explanation anyway.

And really what could she say to him? Oh, by the way, I love you and it breaks my heart to think of you having a child with another woman.

No, she needed space to regain her perspective and come to grips with the fact that no matter what it took, Luke would find a way for his outrageous plan to work. She wasn't part of it.

Walking to the door, she turned. "To borrow one of your favorite phrases when you don't wish to share details…let's just say I feel like taking the time off and leave it at that."

"All right, that's it." As he hung up the phone, Luke sent his desk chair sailing backward and quickly rose to his feet. "I'm going to put an end to this ridiculousness once and for all."

Grabbing his suit jacket from the coat tree, he stuffed his arms into the sleeves and headed for the door. Nothing had gone right since Haley walked out of his office yesterday and she had just called in "sick" for tomorrow. Facing another day with Ruth Ann, the temporary secretary, was completely intolerable and he wanted to know what the hell was going on. He didn't for one damned minute buy Haley's weak excuse that she just didn't feel well.

"I'll be out of the office for the rest of the afternoon, Ruth Ann," Luke growled as he passed the woman seated at Haley's desk. "If you can figure out how, forward all my calls to my cell phone, otherwise just take messages."

"A-all right, Mr. Garnier," she answered in a whiny tone that further irritated him. "W-will there be anything else?"

"No."

Ruth Ann's voice not only resembled the sound of fingernails scraping the surface of a blackboard, she looked and acted as if she was scared to death of him. And that was only scratching the surface of the many problems he had with Haley's temporary replacement.

To say the woman was absolutely incompetent would be the understatement of the year. Ruth Ann couldn't make a decent cup of coffee, couldn't find anything in a simple alphabetic filing system and found the phone to be an utter and complete mystery to her. She somehow reached the public relations coordinator for the Tennessee Titans football team while attempting a conference call with his satellite office in Atlanta.

He needed Haley back on the job immediately. She kept his office running like a well-oiled machine. Not to mention the fact that she made a damned fine cup of coffee.

As Luke navigated the late-afternoon crosstown traffic, he dismissed his current woes with Ruth Ann. He was on his way to find out what the problem was with Haley and believed she would be back on the job the first thing tomorrow morning.

But as he turned the SUV onto the street leading to Haley's apartment complex, his thoughts strayed to his other dilemma. He still needed to find a surrogate. A woman he could trust, as well as have all the qualities he wanted for his heir. And that wasn't going to be easy.

Oh, he knew several women who would be willing to volunteer for the job, and some of them even possessed a few of the traits he wanted for his son. But there wasn't one he could trust to bear him an heir without the benefit of a signed legal agreement. He needed a trustworthy and loyal woman like Haley—one with intelligence and business instincts to match his own. A woman as trustworthy and loyal as Haley. And one who kept herself in good physical condition, was easy on the eyes and enjoyed good health like…Haley.

Parking the Escalade in front of Haley's apartment, Luke took a deep breath before he switched off the engine, exited the SUV and briskly walked to her door. As he pressed the doorbell, he stepped back and waited impatiently for her to answer. When the door swung open, he didn't bother waiting for her to invite him in and brushed right past her into the small living room.

"Luke, what are you doing here?" she asked, looking as surprised as he'd ever seen her.

Smiling, he reached around her and closed the still wide-open door. "I wanted to let you know that I've chosen the perfect surrogate."

"No offense, Luke, but I really don't want to hear anything about this. I don't care who you choose, I just don't want to hear about it," she declared, folding her arms beneath her breasts in a defensive manner.

The action called attention to the size and shape of the pert mounds and the fact that she obviously wasn't wearing a bra. Without a second thought, Luke let his gaze drift lower to her trim waist, shapely hips, then down the length of her long, slender legs.

Damn! If there was ever a woman built for making love, it was Haley Rollins. Odd that he had never noticed how enticing her figure was. Of course, he'd never seen her in a pair of Daisy Duke cutoffs and a hot pink tank top before, either.

As he raised his eyes to her face, he marveled at how feminine she looked. At the office, she always wore her long blond hair straight and most times tied back at the nape of her neck. But today she wore it loose and the soft curls caressed her heart-shaped face and drew attention to her delicate features.

"Luke."

There was a warning in the tone of her soft voice. A warning that he'd never heard before and found completely intriguing. And one that he had every intention of ignoring.

When she impatiently tapped one bare foot, he grinned. "Who are you and what have you done with my business minded executive assistant?"

She glared at him. "I'm not working today, remember? I can wear whatever I like at home. And besides, I wear these when I'm cleaning. Now, would you please tell me why you're here, Luke?"

He grinned. "I've already told you. I've chosen the woman to be my surrogate."

"And you felt compelled to share the news with *me*?"

"Yes."

"Couldn't all this have waited until I returned to the office?"

"I don't see any reason that it should." Walking farther into the room, he shook his head. "I only made my choice a few minutes ago. On the way over here."

"Good for you," she said, sounding less than enthusiastic.

He pointed to her couch. "Have a seat and I'll explain."

"Fine." Clearly running out of patience, she sat and looked up at him expectantly. "Let's get this over with."

"I had several requirements in mind when I made the decision to hire a surrogate. There is only one woman I know who meets all my expectations and who I can trust with something this important," he summarized.

"I know I'm going to be sorry that I asked, but what are you looking for?"

"I want an intelligent woman with excellent business instincts." When it looked as if Haley intended to speak again, he held up his hand to stop her. "I also want her to be reasonably nice looking and in excellent physical condition."

"It sounds to me like you want a superhero," she offered, rolling her eyes.

"I didn't think of it quite that way, but in a sense you might be right," he mused, chuckling at her evaluation. She had no idea that as far as he was concerned she was assessing herself.

He'd always admired Haley's quick wit and he was more confident now than ever that he'd made the right choice. She was definitely the woman he was looking for.

"And you think you've found this paragon?" she prodded.

"Yes." Before she could react, he walked over, took her hands in his and asked, "Haley Rollins, will you have my baby?"

Two

Time stood still and Haley wasn't entirely certain that her heart hadn't come to a complete halt as well. Luke was asking *her* to be his surrogate? He actually wanted her to have his child?

She opened her mouth, closed it, then opened it again as she desperately tried to find her nonexistent voice. The fact that he saw her as the perfect means to produce his heir rendered her utterly speechless.

"I can tell by your reaction that you weren't expecting this," he laughed.

Never in a million years.

"And I don't need your answer right now," he added.

Good. Because that would require words and right now I couldn't put two words together to save my own soul.

He gave her hands a gentle squeeze, then reached for his suit jacket. "I want you to sleep on it tonight and, since you're taking tomorrow off, spend the day thinking about it. I'll pick you up around seven tomorrow evening for dinner. You can give me your answer then."

In a total state of shock, all Haley could do was stare at him. When he pulled her to her feet and led her to the door, she couldn't have protested no matter how hard she tried.

Opening the door, he turned and, reaching out, lightly touched her unruly curls. "By the way, you should wear your hair like this more often. It looks very nice." Then, without another word, he stepped out onto the sidewalk and pulled the door shut.

Haley felt as if she'd fallen down the rabbit hole and landed squarely in the middle of Wonderland. When she'd gotten up yesterday morning, she'd had no idea that in a little over twenty-four hours, her life would take such an unexpected turn. Nor would she have ever thought the man she'd dreamed about for the past five years would get some wild notion that he needed an heir and that she was the only woman to make that happen.

Slowly returning to the couch, she plopped down and let her gaze wander aimlessly around the room. How could everything look the same when the whole world had been turned completely upside down?

As the gravity of Luke's request began to sink in, she shook her head. There was no way on God's green earth that she could help him with his cockamamy plan. She couldn't—wouldn't—do that to a child. To her child.

Her child.

She was pretty sure that, as her father's housekeeper used to say whenever someone expressed a desire to procreate, she had "baby fever." Not because she didn't have plenty of time to have a child. She did.

At twenty-eight years old, she certainly hadn't heard the ominous ticking of her biological clock. Nor did she anticipate that happening for quite some time.

She had, however, watched several of her friends find love, get married and have babies. In fact, just last week Haley had received an announcement from her college roommate about the birth of her second child. And that seemed to intensify the void, her desire that she wanted more than anything else in life—a family of her own.

Just the idea of holding her own baby, of watching him or her take the first steps, of hearing the first words and seeing a sweet toothless grin brought tears to her eyes. She wanted a baby to love and be loved by in return.

But that wasn't what Luke had in mind. He wanted an heir to carry on at Garnier Construction, not a close family who loved, laughed and together weathered whatever storms life sent their way. And she was old-fashioned enough to believe that the choice to conceive should be based on the desire to love and nurture, not a good business decision. If she went along with his ludicrous plan, he'd raise their child alone and she'd be completely out of the picture. She'd lived that type of existence and she couldn't do that to a child, couldn't bring an innocent baby into a childhood like hers. Although the circumstances weren't exactly the same, she knew all too well how it felt to have a workaholic father who always put business first, who relied on nannies and his housekeeper to raise his motherless daughter.

Nor could she do that to herself. Unlike her own mother who abandoned her shortly after birth, nothing would ever keep Haley from being part of her child's life. She had every intention of being there each day to love and guide him or her as they made the journey to a happy, productive adulthood.

Unfortunately, Luke Garnier was a formidable negotiator. She knew as sure as she knew her own name that he would not stop until she agreed to his crazy scheme.

Luckily for her, she knew him well enough to know exactly how to deter him from his mission. But in doing so, it meant effectively ending any romantic fantasies of being more than his glorified secretary. Her chest tightened with intense emotion. It saddened her deeply, but she couldn't see any other option.

Taking a fortifying breath, she rose to her feet and walked into the spare bedroom she'd turned into her home office. As she seated herself at the desk, she took a tablet and pen from the drawer and began compiling her list of conditions. Demands that she was certain Luke would find to be deal-breakers and send him running away from her as fast and far as he could possibly get.

The feel of Luke's hand at the small of her back as the hostess led them to their table sent an interesting little shiver straight up Haley's spine and she focused all her attention on walking it to the table in her three-inch high heels without breaking her neck. Instead of dressing for style, she should have worn a more sensible—and a lot more comfortable—pair of shoes.

But her decision to wear the ridiculous shoes had

been a psychological crutch of sorts. Luke was well over six feet tall and she'd wanted to feel as if she were more on his level. The only problem was, he still towered over her by at least eight inches. So much for trying to psych herself up for their dinner meeting, she thought as they reached the table. All she'd succeeded in doing was to increase the chance of a broken ankle.

When Luke held her chair for her, she noticed that the table was strategically located in a dimly lit corner of the upscale restaurant and gave them a maximum amount of privacy. Knowing Luke, he'd specifically requested it when he made the reservation so they could talk freely without anyone eavesdropping.

"Hello, my name is Martin and I'll be your server for the evening," a young man said as Luke took his seat across from her. "Would you like to see our wine list, Mr. Garnier?"

"That won't be necessary, Martin," Luke answered. He gave her a smile that curled her toes inside her ridiculous shoes as he requested an extremely expensive label and vintage of wine, then added, "We'll both be having the house salad with house dressing. And for the main course we'll have prime rib, baby carrots and asparagus."

Martin nodded. "Good choice, sir. I'll be back in a few moments with your wine."

Haley wasn't at all surprised that Luke had ordered their dinner without consulting her or the menu. That was the type of man he was—a take charge kind of guy, who expected everyone to go along with whatever choices he saw fit to make.

"Did you enjoy your day off?" he asked conversationally, once the young waiter had placed their wine glasses in front of them, then silently moved away. "Were you able to give a significant amount of thought to my request?"

Leave it to him to bypass her need to respond to the small talk and get right to the sole reason they were having dinner together.

"I haven't been able to think of anything else since you left my apartment yesterday afternoon," she said truthfully. "You really gave me a lot to think about."

"Have you reached a decision?"

She stared at his handsome face as she mentally readied herself to recite the list of demands she'd spent the day memorizing and knew would have him rescinding his proposition in less than a heartbeat. But being prepared for what she had to say didn't make saying it any easier.

"Yesterday, when you asked me to consider doing this for you, I don't recall you mentioning anything that would give me an incentive to help you," she clarified, choosing her words carefully. "What would I get out of this besides gaining a significant amount of weight and a few stretch marks?"

"After I left your place, I gave that some thought," he agreed, nodding. "And there's no question that I would take care of all medical expenses, as well as give you as much time off from work as you'd like. With pay, of course."

He made it sound so simple. Had he even considered the permanent changes her body would undergo or the possible risks if the pregnancy was problematic? And what about the emotional devastation she would endure when it came time to give him custody of her child?

"That isn't nearly enough," she declared, flatly. "I want more." She shook her head. "No. That's not correct. I want *a lot* more."

His eyes narrowed and she could tell that he hadn't anticipated her rejection. "What exactly is it you want, Haley?" he finally asked.

"I'm sure it's a lot more than you're willing to give," she stated, taking a sip of wine.

"Name your price and we'll see." There was a challenge in his voice, indicating that he was about to go into serious negotiation mode.

"I never said I wanted money," she offered, staring at him over the rim of her glass.

He cocked one dark eyebrow. "Then what do you want?"

Haley slowly placed her wine goblet on the table and took a deep breath. She was about to reveal the hopes and dreams she'd had since childhood to the man she quite possibly loved, then listen to him reject each and every one of them.

"I don't expect you to understand how I feel about this, but I'm a traditionalist. When I have a baby, I have every intention of being a mother to my child. I'm going to be there to get her up each morning and tuck her into bed each night. I'll be there to see her first steps and hear her first words." She had to pause a moment to keep the emotion out of her voice as she finished. "And every minute of every single day, my child will have the comfort and security of knowing that she's loved and cherished by her mother."

A frown creased his forehead. "Is that it?"

"No."

"There's more?" The lines on his brow deepened and the tone of his voice indicated that he thought she was being extremely unreasonable.

Nodding, she stated the final demand, certain he'd find it completely unacceptable, giving up on her as his surrogate once and for all. "When I have a child, Luke, I intend for her to have a mother and father who are equally responsible for raising her, as well as living under the same roof and sharing the same last name."

His intense stare was intended to intimidate, but as far as she was concerned, this was one issue that was nonnegotiable. He might as well get used to that fact.

"In other words, you want to get married," he said after several uncomfortable moments of silence.

Their waiter chose that moment to bring their salads and she waited for him to leave before she answered. "When I have a baby, yes, I have every intention of being married and making a stable, loving home for my child to grow up in."

"Anything else?"

Shaking her head, she reached for her fork with a trembling hand. "No, I think that just about covers the subject."

Silence reigned over the table as they ate and she knew Luke was contemplating ways to change her mind. But that wasn't going to happen and the sooner he realized it, the better off they'd both be. Then they could forget that he'd even brought up the subject and resume being an executive assistant and her workaholic boss.

"Did you find everything to your satisfaction?" the waiter asked while he removed their plates.

"As always, the meal was excellent," Luke answered. Turning to her, he inquired, "Would you like something for dessert, Haley?"

"No, thank you. I'm positively stuffed." Smiling, she looked up at the server and crossed her fingers beneath the table for the lie she was about to tell. "Everything was delicious."

In truth, she couldn't have said whether they'd had prime rib or a piece of shoe leather. She'd been far too preoccupied wondering when Luke would tell her that he found her requirements completely unacceptable and that he was officially deleting her from his short list of surrogacy candidates.

Nodding, Luke handed the waiter a credit card. "I think that will be it for this evening. Have the valet bring my car around to the front."

Once Luke had taken care of the check and they walked out of the restaurant, they had very little to say to each other. The drive home was little better and Haley was more than relieved when he parked the car, walked her to her door and bid her a very quick, very platonic good-night.

Confident that he'd given up on the idea of her becoming the surrogate for his child, Haley felt her mood dip into sadness. When she'd told Luke what she wanted, she'd been revealing the dreams she'd carried for the past five years. And knowing there wasn't a snowball's chance on a hot July day that any of them would come true now, was almost enough to send her running to the freezer for the carton of triple fudge nut ice cream she kept on hand for just such depressing occasions. Instead, she opted to change into her nightshirt, pour herself a small glass of white wine and watch the nightly news on television before turning in for the evening.

But half an hour later, as she crawled beneath the sheets on her bed and reached to turn off her bedside lamp, the phone rang. The caller ID revealed Luke's cell number and her heart skittered to a stop.

This is it, she thought, taking a deep fortifying breath. He was calling to tell her that he found her requirements totally unacceptable and he would be searching elsewhere for his surrogate.

"Hello, Luke."

"Have you already gone to bed?" His deep baritone sounded so darned smooth and sexy it sent tiny little shivers straight up her spine.

"Uh…yes, but I hadn't gone to sleep."

"Good. Get out of bed and get to the front door."

Her scalp tingled and a wave of goose bumps shimmered over her arms. "Why?"

"Because I'll be there in about thirty seconds and I want to get this thing settled tonight."

"Can't we discuss this over the phone?" she asked, throwing back the covers and scrambling out of bed. Holding the phone between her shoulder and ear, she frantically searched for her robe. Where on earth had she put the thing? She rarely wore it because she never had overnight visitors.

"No, I'd rather talk in person," he said as the doorbell rang. "Now, open the door and let me in, Haley."

At the sound of him ending the call, she tossed the phone on her bed and, giving up on finding her robe, pulled her raincoat out of the closet. "All right, I'm coming," she muttered when the bell rang again. Shrugging into the coat, she hurried down the hall to the entryway. "Somebody needs to remind Mr. Luke Garnier that patience is a virtue."

When she opened the door, Luke walked right in as he'd done the day before. "Are you going out?" he inquired, turning to eye her coat.

Pushing the door closed, she pulled the coat's belt tight around her waist. "I couldn't find my bathrobe and you wouldn't stop ringing the doorbell."

"You don't keep your robe handy?" he asked as he walked into the living room.

"I live alone and if I want to walk around without a robe, there's no one here to care," she replied, wondering why she bothered to explain herself. It was her business, not his. "Now, what do we need to discuss that can't wait until tomorrow morning, Luke? I thought I made my position quite clear at dinner."

"You did," he said, nodding. "And I've given it a fair amount of thought."

She couldn't tell what he was thinking from his expression, but knowing him, he was there to get her to come around to his way of thinking. "I'm not changing my mind, Luke."

"I didn't think you would." Staring at her, he took a deep breath.

Here it comes, she thought, anticipating his rejection of her requirements.

"I've decided that the terms you laid down tonight are within reason and I'm willing to accept them," he stated as if closing a business deal.

Her heart felt as if it lodged in her throat at the same time her knees gave way. Sinking down on the couch, she could have sworn that the walls started to move in on her.

"W-what did you say?"

"We'll get married this weekend right after you sign a prenuptial agreement covering the protection of my assets, shared custody of my heir and a fair settlement for you if and when the marriage ends."

"But…we…I mean, you—"

"I assume that since you haven't indicated otherwise, you'll be in the office tomorrow morning?" he interrupted.

Unable to find her voice for the second time in as many days, all she could manage was a short nod.

"We can discuss the details and refine our agreement then," he continued. "Now, get some sleep. We have a big day ahead of us."

Haley watched him walk to the door, then close it with a click that seemed to echo throughout the room. She couldn't move, couldn't speak and rational thought was completely out of the question.

What on earth just happened? Had her commitment-phobic boss really just informed her that they would be getting married for the sole purpose of having a baby? And this weekend, no less?

Knowing that sleep would be out of the question, she took off her raincoat and tossed it on the back of the couch. As she prowled the room like a caged tiger, she tried to arrange her tangled thoughts into some semblance of order.

The man of her dreams, the very man who clearly stated he had no time for love and marriage, was willing to become her husband. And his only purpose for making her his wife wasn't because he loved her and wanted to raise a family with her. He was willing to marry her in order to have her bear him an heir.

She stopped in the middle of the room and barely suppressed a scream. Every one of her dreams was well on the way to becoming reality and for all the wrong reasons.

She wanted love and all the bonding that went with it. She wanted a lifetime emotional commitment, not a prenuptial agreement. But to Luke, their union would be just another business arrangement.

As she stood there, she couldn't help but wonder where her plan had gone wrong. And what had possessed him to agree to her demands?

But most important of all, how in the name of all that was holy was she going to talk him out of following through with it?

Three

The next morning, Luke slid a folder across his desk for Haley's perusal. "I've taken the liberty of having an attorney who specializes in family law draw up a pre-nuptial contract for you to sign."

"How did you manage to get this done so quickly?" she asked, looking a lot like the proverbial deer caught in the headlights of a car.

"You can get just about anything done in a short amount of time for the right price." He nodded toward the document she hadn't yet touched. "I think you'll find the agreement spells out what is expected from both of us when it comes to joint custody and parenting the boy. It also covers what we'll both keep and what compensation you'll receive when the marriage is dissolved."

She looked a little distressed. "And when will that be?"

"Whenever we both agree that we'd like to move on with our lives." He shrugged. "I'm sure we'll know when the time comes." Leaning back in his chair, he motioned toward the folder. "Take your time to read over the contract, then sign it and have it back on my desk by the end of the day."

"It's so generous of you to give me an ample amount of time to think over what I'll be signing," she said, her tone sarcastic.

He stated what he saw as obvious. "I don't intend to drag my feet on getting this finalized. You laid down the terms, I've made the decision to comply with them and we'll get married on Saturday morning. But between now and then we have a lot to do."

"What's the rush?" she asked, hiding a yawn behind her delicate hand. She looked thoroughly exhausted and he'd bet his next multimillion-dollar deal that she hadn't slept a wink the night before. The thought that she'd soon be in his bed caused his heart to stall and a slow smile to tug at the corners of his mouth.

"Why wait?" he responded, answering her question with one of his own. "I want to get started making you pregnant as soon as possible." That instantly brought her fully awake and added quite a bit of color to her unusually pale cheeks.

"You can't be serious. We'll be sleeping together?" She shook her head and the curls brushing her flawless cheeks fascinated the hell out of him. "I don't remember you mentioning anything about that last night."

He smiled. The idea of waking up with her in his arms each morning was becoming more appealing with each passing second. "I didn't think I'd have to. The last I heard, that's what married people do."

Her turquoise eyes grew wide. "But the only reason for the marriage is to have a child. I thought we'd be sleeping in separate rooms and visit a doctor for some kind of medical procedure. That's what we would be doing if we weren't getting married."

"You assumed wrong." He couldn't stop himself from giving her a wicked grin. "I have all of the required equipment, sweetheart. And let me assure you, everything works just fine. I see no reason for us to resort to a turkey baster when I'm perfectly capable of taking care of the job myself."

He almost laughed out loud at the shocked expression crossing her pretty face. "But we barely even know each other outside of this office. And you've made it quite clear that you have no expectations of the marriage lasting for any length of time after the birth."

Had he heard a hint of panic in her voice?

Interesting.

"That's not exactly true. I said we'd know when it was time to move on. That could be a month, a year or even ten years after the birth before that happens. But that's not the point," he said, shaking his head. "I can't think of a better way to get acquainted than making love. Besides, if I have to get married to get the heir I want, you can damned well bet I'm going to enjoy all of the benefits of the marital institution. And that includes sleeping with you." Heat began to gather in his lower belly and anticipation filled his chest. There were definite advantages to meeting her demands.

He didn't think it was possible, but the blush on her

cheeks changed from pink to a deep rose. Was it possible that Haley found the idea of making love with him less than appealing? Or could it be that she was a bit more innocent than he'd anticipated?

Deciding to find out, he stood up and rounding the desk, took her by the hand to help her to her feet. "While you read and sign the prenup, I'll make the arrangements for our trip to Pigeon Forge," he said, taking her into his arms.

"W-what are you doing?"

"Giving the woman I'm going to marry a hug," he responded, drawing her a bit closer. Holding her to him increased the heat in his lower body and sent a shaft of excitement straight through him.

At first, she stood stiffly in his arms. "We aren't going...to be married...here in Nashville?" she asked, sounding delightfully breathless.

"No."

When he drew her even closer, Luke felt a tiny tremor course through Haley and instantly knew his suspicions about her innocence were right on the mark. He normally liked his women to be a little more experienced. But for reasons he couldn't put his finger on, he found Haley's inexperience oddly touching.

"I have an important meeting with the management employees of Laurel Enterprises and I want to tour my new properties and meet the construction crews," he explained, enjoying the feel of her silky hair against his cheek. "And since there are several wedding chapels in the Pigeon Forge area where we'll be staying, it just makes sense for us to get married while we're there."

"This is a..." She paused. "...huge step. I'm not

entirely certain we're doing the right thing. Are you sure you want to go through with this?"

"I am."

"Really?" She didn't sound as if she believed him for a minute.

He nodded. "You told me that it would take us getting married before you'd have my son and I'm complying. In some courts, a verbal agreement is as binding as any contract. And unless you've changed your mind about us being married, I'd say we have a solid deal, sweetheart."

"No, I haven't changed my mind."

He smiled. "I didn't think so." Releasing her, before she realized just how much he looked forward to making her pregnant the old-fashioned way, he picked up the folder containing the prenuptial agreement. "This is fairly basic and straightforward. After you sign it, I want you to take the rest of the day off, as well as tomorrow."

"Why?" she asked, looking confused. "I thought you said we had a lot to accomplish."

He nodded again. "I need to review the agenda for my meeting with the Laurel employees, call the charter service to arrange our flight and reserve a wedding chapel for the ceremony."

"But you normally have me make those arrangements for you."

"You'll be too busy."

She frowned. "Doing what?"

"You'll need to pack, inform management that you're giving up your apartment and decide whether to store your furniture or donate it to an agency for the homeless." He walked back around the desk and reaching for his suit jacket hanging on the back of his chair, removed his wallet. "I almost forgot. I have to attend a charity thing at one of the museums tomorrow evening and I need a date. I want you to go shopping for something new to wear," he said, handing her one of his credit cards. "And while you're at it, you might as well get whatever you're going to wear for the marriage ceremony on Saturday."

To his amazement, she looked as if he'd offered her a poisonous snake instead of the small harmless piece of plastic. "If I want something new to wear, I'll get it myself." She sounded more than a little offended as she scooped up the folder containing the prenup. "For your information, Mr. Garnier, I'm not destitute. You pay me more than enough to be able to afford whatever clothes I wish to purchase."

As he watched her leave his office in an obvious huff, he wondered what he'd said to upset her. Didn't men buy things for their spouses anymore?

Of course, he and Haley weren't married yet. Maybe she took exception to him paying for things like that before they'd made their union official.

But the way he saw it, it was already a done deal. They had a verbal agreement, would soon have a signed prenup and within a few days a marriage certificate. End of story.

Staring at his computer screen, Luke still couldn't quite believe that in two days, he'd be a married man. Hell, he'd spent the better part of his adult life avoiding anything more than a casual relationship with any woman. And he'd never so much as entertained the idea of getting married. So why was he jumping into the deep end of the marital pool with both feet now?

Haley had every trait he wanted for his heir—intelligence, a good head for business and excellent health. And for another, he couldn't get her to have his son without the benefit of marriage. Yet, when he'd first heard her requirements to agree to his plan, he'd rejected the idea outright and given serious consideration to looking for a different woman. But the more he'd thought about it over the course of their dinner together, then later on the drive to his place after dropping her off at her apartment, the more sense it made and the more appeal it held.

She was extremely passionate about mothering a child and that would definitely work to his benefit. He had several satellite offices throughout the south, requiring a certain amount of travel, and juggling a small child with all the paraphernalia required for his care would be counterproductive. Besides, he would have had to hire a nanny to care for his son until the boy was out of infancy and old enough to go with him to the actual job sites anyway. But with Haley sharing custody of the child, Luke wouldn't have to worry about finding someone suitable to give his son the quality of care he expected.

And then there was the more pleasurable aspect of marriage. Until he'd stopped by to ask her to be his surrogate, Luke had never seen Haley outside of the office and certainly not wearing anything other than the conservative suits she seemed to prefer for her job.

But when she'd opened her door and he caught sight of her long, slender legs in those extremely short little cutoffs and the size and shape of her pert breasts in that snug tank top, it had damn-near knocked his socks off. It had been like he was seeing her for the very first time and every one of his male instincts had come to full attention—reminding him in the most basic of ways that he hadn't had the pleasure of a woman's company in his bed for a very long time.

His lower body tightened even more. In two short days, Haley would be his and he would be making love to her quite frequently. Just the thought of having those shapely legs wrapped around him and her soft body cradling his caused the heat deep in the pit of his belly to flicker into a flame.

"Here's your signed prenup," Haley said, choosing that moment to walk into his office. When she tossed the folder onto his desk, then turned to leave, she added, "And unless you wish to issue another edict about what I need to do before we make the trip to Pigeon Forge, I'll be leaving the office now."

So that was why she'd become so upset. She obviously viewed his suggestions about her apartment and buying something new to wear as high-handedness. He'd have to remember that calling all the shots at the office was one thing, but he'd have to exercise a little more diplomacy when they were discussing what he thought she should do in her personal life.

"Before you leave there's just one more thing. Are you using anything for birth control?" He knew she wasn't presently seeing anyone, but that didn't mean she wasn't prepared.

Her cheeks colored the pretty shade of rose they always did when he mentioned anything to do with sex. "No. That's not an issue."

"Good."

"Is there anything else?" she asked, her gaze not quite meeting his.

"I'm pretty sure what I told you earlier covers everything," he said, unable to stand up without her seeing the evidence of his arousal. "I'll give you a call this evening to let you know what time I'll pick you up for the charity event tomorrow evening."

She shrugged one slender shoulder as she continued toward the door. "Whatever."

"Haley?" When she stopped and turned to face him, he grinned. "There is one more thing I really think you should consider doing."

"What?"

Her withering glare might have stopped a lesser man, but it didn't phase Luke one damned bit. Nor did it stop him from a little teasing.

"Be sure to get plenty of rest between now and Saturday." He gave her a suggestive wink. "I plan on getting our little project started this weekend."

When her cheeks turned bright pink and she fled his office like something chased her, he laughed out loud. Getting married just might prove to be more fun than he'd first thought. At least temporarily.

As Luke held her hand to help her out of his limousine, Haley glanced at the other couples arriving for the museum's annual charity event. She recognized several prominent businessmen, a couple of them Luke's rivals, and she knew they were attending for the same reason Luke was—meeting potential clients. Making a contact at a social function could mean the difference between signing a lucrative contract to build the next high-rise to grace the Nashville skyline or watching the competition walk away with the job.

"It's good to see you again, Luke," a distinguished-looking elderly gentleman greeted them as they walked through the museum's entrance. He pumped Luke's hand, then turned to give her a friendly smile. "And who is this lovely young lady?"

"My executive assistant, Haley Rollins," Luke answered, already scanning the crowd in the atrium. "Haley, I'd like for you to meet Max Parmelli, the curator of the museum and the head of this year's charity drive for the city's homeless shelters."

Holding her hand, the older man leaned forward to kiss the back of it. "It's a real pleasure to meet you, Ms. Rollins."

She smiled at the pleasant older man, but Luke prevented any other greeting when he placed his hand to her back and guided her through the crowd toward a group of men standing by the fountain in the middle of the room. One of them she recognized as a former client of Garnier Construction who she knew in the very near future was going to be expanding his current building, if not contracting for a new one.

"Why don't you look at some of the exhibits or get something for yourself at the buffet tables?" Luke advised, his attention clearly focused on the men by the fountain. "I'll find you in a few minutes."

Effectively dismissed, she watched him join the group before heading toward a display of artifacts believed to belong to the ill-fated Romanov family of Russia. She really wasn't all that interested in any of the exhibits, but she couldn't—wouldn't—just stand there like a little lost puppy, waiting for Luke to once again grace her with his attention.

Sighing, she wandered around the museum, wondering what on earth she'd gotten herself into. It hadn't been lost on her that Luke had introduced her to the curator as his executive assistant, instead of his fiancée or future wife. Nor did he have any compunction about dumping her in favor of soliciting a possible repeat client.

But she really didn't have any reason to complain. He'd made it quite clear that he was only marrying her because he couldn't get her to have his heir any other way. And she was going through with their arrangement because she wanted a baby more than she'd ever wanted anything in her entire life.

Haley smiled as she absently gazed at a delicate, elaborately decorated egg. She was finally going to have her own baby—a child she would love and nurture and who would love her unconditionally in return. And the fact that Luke was going to be the baby's daddy made her decision to go through with their agreement much easier. The only fly in the ointment was the fact that Luke didn't love her, nor did he make any pretense that he expected their marriage to last.

"It looks pretty fragile, doesn't it?"

At the sound of the male voice at her shoulder, Haley turned to find a nice-looking man with dark blond hair and sparkling green eyes standing next to her. "Yes, it does," she said, really taking a look at the Faberge egg in the glass case in front of her for the first time.

"Back where I come from, we fry up the eggs for breakfast and throw the shells away," he remarked, laughing.

"And home is Oklahoma or Texas?" she asked, recognizing his southwestern drawl.

"Beaver, Oklahoma, to be exact," he announced proudly.

"And you?"

"I was born and raised in Atlanta." She walked to the next display case containing pictures of the Romanov family shortly before their deaths. "But I've lived in Nashville since I was in college."

"Never went to college myself," the man disclosed, shaking his head as he followed her. "I left home right after graduating high school with a fifty dollar bill in my pocket and an old guitar slung over my shoulder." He grinned. "That was fifteen years ago and I've been here ever since."

"So you're in the music business?" she asked politely.

The man looked shocked for a moment before giving her a wide grin. "You're about the sweetest thing I've come across in a long time. What's your name, darlin'?"

She caught sight of Luke coming toward them like a charging bull. "Haley, I need you to come with me." The censure she detected in his voice startled her.

"Haley is it?" the man beside her repeated, smiling. "Pretty name for a pretty lady."

She ignored the man's compliment as Luke came to stand on the other side of her. "Is something wrong?"

"No. I just want to get your opinion on one of the paintings offered here that I thought would make a nice addition to the office." Before she could respond, he glared at the friendly man standing beside her. "You'll have to excuse us."

When Luke took her by the elbow and strongly urged her in the opposite direction, she gave the man an apologetic smile. "It was nice talking with you."

He nodded. "You, too, Haley. That's just my luck, though. All the pretty ones are already spoke for."

She frowned as Luke hurried her toward a gallery on the opposite side of the atrium. "Are you sure there's nothing wrong?"

"We'll talk about it later," he said, leading her to an abstract painting. "Right now, I want your opinion on this. Do you think this would be appropriate for the reception area?"

She stared at him before she finally shook her head and turned her attention to the painting. "I'm not the person you should be asking about this."

He looked surprised. "Why not?"

"Because I prefer a more realistic rendering," she elaborated, pointing to a beautiful landscape down the long wall. "I especially love scenes like this."

"Really?" Shaking his head, he glanced from one painting to the other. "I wouldn't have guessed that about you."

"I'm sure there's a lot about me you'd never guess," she murmured, moving on to view another canvas. If he was surprised by her taste in artwork, he'd be shocked right down to his Italian loafers to learn how she truly felt about him.

While Luke arranged the purchase and delivery of the landscape she had chosen for the Garnier office on Monday, Haley continued looking at the array of artwork.

"You know, that picture looks like something my

nephew did when he was in kindergarten," a familiar voice remarked from behind her.

Turning, Haley smiled at the man she'd talked to earlier in the room displaying the Romanov treasures. "You wouldn't happen to be following me, would you?"

He grinned. "Would it bother you if I said yes?"

"It wouldn't set well with me."

Haley glanced up to see Luke walking toward them, his expression anything but pleased. "Come on, Haley. It's time I took you home."

"There you go again, trying to steal her away from me," the man said good-naturedly.

Luke placed his hand to her back. "Pal, she's not yours for me to steal away. She's already mine and you might as well give up the chase. It's not going to happen tonight or any other night."

Surprised by his possessive words, Haley didn't even think to protest as Luke guided her to the exit. But when they stepped onto the sidewalk in front of the museum and she finally found her voice, she asked "What was that all about?"

He gave the valet instructions to call for his limo before turning to face her. "Do you even know who you were talking to?"

"No. Why?"

Luke's frown eased a bit. "That was country music's bad boy, Chet Parker. Surely you've heard about his womanizing. He has quite a reputation."

She glanced over her shoulder at the museum's entrance. "You can't be serious," she said, amazed that she hadn't recognized the country music superstar.

"He's divorced again," Luke advised disgustedly.

"And I'd say he was sizing you up as his next candidate."

Haley shook her head. "I doubt that. We were just chatting about the displays."

"Guys like Parker don't strike up a casual conversation with a woman. Not without an ulterior motive." When his limousine pulled up to the curb, Luke helped her into the back, then slid in beside her. "Just keep in mind that you and I have a deal. And it doesn't include the likes of Chet Parker."

A mixture of anger and disappointment settled in the pit of Haley's stomach. Luke wasn't acting possessive because he cared for her, he was just concerned that she might find a reason to renege on their agreement.

Thankful the ride to her place was short, when the driver parked the car in front of her apartment, she gathered her evening bag and readied herself to escape Luke's presence. If she didn't, she wasn't entirely certain she wouldn't bop him on top of his thick head with her sequined clutch.

Unfortunately, he had other ideas. When the chauffer opened the door and Luke got out to help her to her feet, he wrapped his arm around her waist and started up the walk to her door.

"There's no need to see me inside. I'm perfectly capable of finding my own way."

"I'm sure you can," he said as he continued to escort her to the front step. Taking her key from her, he fit it into the lock and opened her door. "But I always make sure my date gets inside safely."

"Your date? I wasn't aware that's what I was tonight," she retorted, unable to stop herself.

"Of course you were."

She shook her head. "Let me see. You didn't ask me to go to the event with you, you told me that we were going. Then this evening, I was introduced as your executive assistant and immediately dismissed in favor of a potential client. And at no time during the evening do I remember you referring to me as your date or being treated like one, unless you want to count that little display of macho possessiveness with Chet Parker."

He looked at her like he didn't have a clue what she was talking about. "You are my assistant and I'm sure you recognized the client I was talking with. I don't need to tell you how profitable his business could be for Garnier Construction. And as far as Parker was concerned, he needed to get the message that you're unavailable."

Suddenly too tired to explain what he was obviously missing, she reached for her key. "On second thought, just forget it. You probably wouldn't understand if I drew you a picture."

"Oh, I get it." He held her key just out of reach. "You feel that I neglected you this evening."

"No," she lied. That was exactly the way she'd felt, but for one thing, he had no idea that she had romantic feelings for him. And for another, he didn't see her as anything more than his executive assistant, who had obviously lost her mind and agreed to help him with his cockamamy scheme to have a baby.

"Please, give me my key. I'll see you tomorrow morning when you pick me up to go to Pigeon Forge," she responded, holding out her hand.

To her surprise, he shook his head and wrapped his arms around her waist to draw her to him. "I can't let you think that I was ignoring you." He smiled as he ran his index finger over the scooped neckline of her dress. "Or that I didn't notice how sexy you look in this little black number."

Haley felt as if her heart bounced down to the pit of her stomach, then rebounded to lodge in her throat. His strong arms holding her securely to his tall, solid frame and the intention in his dark blue gaze sent a shiver of sheer delight through her. How many times in the past several years had she imagined him looking at her that way? Or what it would feel like to be in his arms and have him kiss her?

But when he lowered his head to cover her mouth with his, reality far exceeded any of her fantasies. Light and tender, his firm lips moved over hers with such care it robbed her of breath and sent a delicious warmth flowing in her body.

Tingles of excitement rushed through her when he used his tongue to coax her mouth to open for him. Haley couldn't have denied him access to her inner recesses if her life depended on it. She wanted to experience every nuance of Luke's kiss, wanted to taste him and have him taste her in return.

As his tongue mated with hers, her knees gave way and she raised her arms to his shoulders to keep from falling. Never had a kiss left her feeling as if every bone in her body had been turned to soft, malleable putty.

But all too soon Luke eased the pressure of his mouth on hers and nibbled tiny kisses from her lips to her ear, then down to the hollow below. "I'll be by around seven in the morning to get you," he whispered, sending a wave of heat coursing through her.

"Th-that's awfully early," she noted, distracted by his warm breath feathering over her suddenly sensitive skin.

"I want to get the wedding out of the way before I meet with the Laurel employees," he stated, releasing her to step back.

Being doused with a bucket of ice water couldn't have been more effective in ending the sensual feelings he'd created within her. Of course he'd think of their wedding as an inconvenience to be dispensed with as quickly as possible in order to get back to business as usual.

"Don't bother," she said, plucking her key from his fingers. "I'll meet you at the airfield."

Walking into her apartment and closing the door before he could argue the point further, Haley barely suppressed the urge to scream. She hadn't expected him to feel the same about their wedding as she did. After all, she might love him, but he barely knew she existed beyond the office. Yet, it certainly would have been nice for him to view the ceremony as more than just fulfilling one of the details of their agreement.

She shook her head as she entered her bedroom to change into her nightgown. Her father's housekeeper used to warn her to be careful what she wished for because she just might get it.

Haley had never understood what the woman meant more than she did at that very moment. Tomorrow she would have everything she'd wished for. She would become Luke Garnier's wife—albeit temporarily—and quite possibly within the next year, the mother of his child.

So why wasn't she happier about it? And why did she feel like she was embarking on a journey that could very well end up destroying her?

Four

The following morning, barely an hour after they were picked up by a limousine at the Knoxville airport, Haley walked down the aisle of a little log wedding chapel in Pigeon Forge toward Luke and the rotund minister waiting to unite them in holy matrimony. Dressed in a black pin-striped suit, pearl gray shirt and burgundy tie, Luke looked as handsome and confident as she had ever remembered seeing him. And within a few short minutes, they would be husband and wife.

Unbelievable.

After all these years, the man of her dreams had finally seen her as more than his glorified secretary. The only problem was, when he finally did take a second glance in her direction, all he'd been able to see was a fertile egg and an incubator.

When she reached the end of the aisle and stopped beside Luke, the grandfatherly minister smiled. "Please turn to face one another and join hands."

Haley was sure she stopped breathing when Luke captured her hands in his and smiled down at her. His encouraging expression and the feel of his solid palms against hers sent tingles rippling up her spine and reminded her that later on that evening, she'd feel those same strong hands elsewhere on her body, exploring, caressing, teasing.

"Are you ready to put the final touch on this deal?" he asked, completely unaware of the direction her thoughts had taken her.

"I…um, suppose I am," she murmured, not at all surprised that he refused to acknowledge their marriage as anything more than one of his business agreements.

"Good. The meeting with the Laurel people is due to start in…" he glanced at his watch "…a little less than forty-five minutes."

"Of course." She glared at him and before she could stop herself, added, "I couldn't possibly expect you to keep them waiting for something as trivial as your own wedding."

Frowning, Luke looked at her like she'd sprouted another head. "You knew that I'd scheduled the meeting for today."

Didn't he realize that no matter the reason for a marriage, a woman's wedding day was special to her? That having the groom rush off to a business meeting immediately following the ceremony wasn't exactly the stuff a woman's dreams were made of?

"It doesn't matter," she said, resigned that he would never understand.

His smile faded and clearing his throat, the minister interrupted their verbal sparring to ask "Are y'all real sure you folks want to go through with this wedding?"

"Yes," Luke declared, his tone leaving no doubt he meant it.

When the man turned his attention her way, she glanced up at Luke. Even though she was keenly disappointed over his insensitivity, the time for backing out of this fiasco had come and gone. She'd given her word and that was something she tried never to go back on. Besides, she wanted a baby—his baby—more than she'd ever wanted anything and she wasn't going to pass up the opportunity for the child she wanted to be that of the man of her dreams.

"Yes, I want to marry him," she admitted, surprised by the surety in her own voice.

"All right, I guess if you're both agreeable, we'll get started then," the minister indicated, sounding more than a little doubtful as he opened his book of wedding vows. "We are gathered here today to join this man and this woman in the bonds of—"

Staring at Luke, she heard very little of the blessedly brief ceremony and was surprised when the minister asked, "Do you have a wedding ring for your bride, son?"

Luke frowned. "No."

"It's really not that important anyway," she said, hoping her voice didn't reflect her disillusionment.

She didn't know if Luke had forgotten about a ring for her or if he purposely hadn't bought one. But either way, it was one more detail about her wedding day that she'd just as soon forget.

The man raised one bushy gray eyebrow, then shaking his head turned to the groom. "Luke, do you take Haley to be your lawful wedded wife, to have and to hold, for richer or poorer, in sickness and in health, as long as you both shall live?"

There wasn't even the slightest hesitation in his rich baritone when Luke gazed into her eyes and answered, "I do."

The minister nodded, then turned to her. "And Haley, do you take Luke to be your lawful wedded husband, to have and to hold, for richer or poorer, in sickness and in health, as long as you both shall live?"

"I…uh…yes. Yes, I do." Knowing their marriage was only a temporary arrangement, she hated making a vow she knew for certain wouldn't be kept.

As if he couldn't quite believe what he was about to say, the minister shook his head as he announced, "Then by the power vested in me by Sevier County and the great state of Tennessee, I now pronounce you husband and wife." He gave Luke a questioning look. "Son, if you want to kiss your bride, now would be the time to give it a try."

For the briefest of moments, as she watched Luke lower his head, she thought he was going to brush her lips with his and that would be the end of it. But the light of challenge she detected in his intense gaze a split second before he wrapped his arms around her and pulled her to him, warned her that the kiss was going to be anything but casual or brief.

Haley caught her breath and when his mouth settled

over hers, every cell in her body seemed to zing to life. At first, his firm, warm lips moved over hers with such tender care, such thoughtfulness, she felt as if she might just melt into a puddle right there on the chapel floor. But when he tightened his arms and pressed her even closer, her heart began an erratic cadence and a current of electrified heat coursed from the top of her head all the way to the tips of her toes.

The feel of his solid body against her much softer one as he coaxed her mouth to open for him caused an interesting little swirl in the most feminine part of her and Haley didn't have the presence of mind to put up so much as a token protest. Allowing him access, she leaned into him as he stroked and teased. But when he engaged her tongue in a game of advance and retreat, she felt as if her knees had turned to rubber and she wrapped her arms around his trim waist to keep from falling in an undignified heap at his feet.

She'd been kissed many times before, but never like this, never with such tenderness and purpose. Not even their first kiss had affected her as profoundly, and by the time Luke eased away from the caress, Haley felt completely and irrevocably claimed.

She silently stood by Luke's side as the chapel's photographer snapped several pictures, then handed him the disk of still shots and a DVD of the ceremony, along with their newly signed marriage certificate.

"Thank you," Haley murmured as Luke took her hand in his and led her up the aisle and out of the chapel door to their waiting limo.

"I've got to hurry to make the meeting with the Laurel employees on time," he said, helping her into the backseat of the long black car. When he slid in beside her on the plush leather seat, he checked his watch, then tapped on the window separating them from the driver. "Take me directly to the Laurel Enterprises office in Gatlinburg, then drive Ms. Rollins up to the Mountain Crest Lodge."

"You don't want me to attend the meeting with you?" Since she was his executive assistant, she'd been included in several employee meetings in the past and she'd assumed that would be the case this time.

He shook his head. "Besides meeting with the office staff, I'll be touring a couple of job sites and talking to the work crews. But I plan to be back in time for dinner this evening."

"Will I need to go shopping for food?" At least buying a few groceries and preparing a meal would give her something to fill the empty hours of the long day ahead.

"No. I've arranged for a caterer to make dinner for us. And the housekeeper will oversee the clean-up in the kitchen before she leaves for the evening."

After college, Haley had done her own cooking and cleaning and liked it that way. Having someone perform those duties for her again was going to take some getting used to.

It took a moment for her to realize that the car had stopped in the parking lot of Laurel Enterprises on the outskirts of Gatlinburg. As with most of the other buildings in the area, it was a log structure that complimented the surrounding environment, instead of detracting from it.

"What am I supposed to do for the rest of the day?"

Being abandoned by her new husband right after they exchanged vows, then sequestered in a mountaintop lodge with nothing to do wasn't exactly the way she'd dreamed her wedding day would unfold.

"It's a nice spring day. You could sit on one of the decks and enjoy the view of Mount LeConte," he said, waiting for their driver to open his door. "Or you could spend the afternoon relaxing in the hot tub." He started to get out of the car, then turned back. "But whatever else you decide to do, make sure that you get plenty of rest." Giving her a quick kiss and a smile that spoke volumes, he winked. "If you'll remember, we're going to start making a baby tonight."

All the way up the mountain to the lodge where they would be staying, Haley tried to remind herself that her marriage to Luke was one of convenience. He viewed their union as the means to an end—a way to get the heir he wanted.

But no matter how hard she tried, she couldn't help but resent the fact that he wasn't even willing to take their wedding day off from work. Nor could she stop a keen sense of sadness from filling her. She'd always envisioned having a baby with a man who loved her and was as devoted to her and their child as she intended to be.

And although she'd known and accepted that theirs was a one-sided relationship, that knowledge did very little to help her stifle an almost uncontrollable urge to let the flood gates open and have herself a good cleansing cry. Nor did it keep her from wanting to tell the driver to turn around and take her back to Nashville and the safe haven of her comfortable little apartment.

* * *

Long after the limousine driver let him out in front of the Mountain Crest Lodge and drove back down the mountain, Luke stood staring at the dark windows of the huge three-story log structure. Haley hadn't bothered leaving a light on for him and he couldn't say that he blamed her. Hurrying off immediately after the wedding ceremony to meet with the Laurel people, he'd left her to fend for herself on their wedding day. That was probably more than enough to get him nominated for jerk of the year.

He checked his watch. It was well past midnight and he'd missed most of his own wedding night as well. He didn't pretend to be an expert on the subject by any means, but even he knew that kind of behavior fell short of what was expected of a newly married man. And especially one who had wed for the sole purpose of making his partner pregnant. But the truth of the matter was, he hadn't expected the intensity of his reaction to Haley when he'd watched her walk down the aisle toward him or the emotions that he'd experienced during the ceremony. Wearing a simple, sleeveless white dress and with her hair in that curly style he'd liked the day he stopped by her apartment, she had been absolutely stunning. And he still had a hard time believing that in the five years she'd worked for him, he hadn't once taken notice of how beautiful she was.

But it was when she'd looked up at him with those trusting turquoise eyes, that a need to protect and take care of her threatened to overwhelm him.

And if that wasn't enough to throw him for a loop, the kiss they'd shared at the end of the brief ceremony was. When he'd kissed her the night before, it had been quite promising and more than a little pleasant. But it couldn't compare to the kiss they'd shared to seal their vows. The feel of her soft, sweet lips beneath his and the need to possess her had been staggering. He'd never in his entire thirty-six years experienced anything even close to that with any other woman.

That was what sent him rushing off to meet the Laurel people. He'd needed the distance to regain his perspective on the matter.

Unfortunately, the meeting ran a lot longer than he anticipated, then he'd learned of a labor dispute that threatened to shut down work on several job sites. By the time he'd straightened out the problem so that the jobs could resume the next week, it was well after midnight. And if missing the wedding dinner he'd arranged for them and not being there to make love to Haley on their wedding night didn't lock up the prize jerk award for him, he didn't know what would.

He sighed heavily as he started up the steps to the front door of the lodge. As he keyed in the security code and opened the door, he wondered if she would honor their agreement of having his child. But as he walked through the great room on his way to the master suite, he shook his head. There was no doubt in his mind that Haley would hold up her end of the arrangement. If there was one thing he knew about his executive assistant, it was that her word was as good as any signed contract. And he'd known from the minute she'd outlined her conditions that if he accepted her criteria, she'd go through with it.

Still, that didn't change the fact that she probably expected a lot more from him on their wedding day.

Luke narrowed his eyes at the sight of his big empty bed. The comforter was still in place, indicating no one had been in it. He looked around the room and noted that her overnight case was nowhere in sight.

Where the hell was she?

His strides purposeful, he crossed the great room and taking the stairs two at a time, went in search of his wayward assistant. There were seven other bedrooms in the place and Haley had damned well better be in one of them.

By the time he got to the door at the end of the hall, Luke was already planning to call the housekeeper and put the woman through the third degree about when Haley had left and if she'd indicated where she was going. But when he glanced in the last bedroom, his irritation instantly disappeared at the sight before him.

The moonlight streaming through the floor-to-ceiling windows bathed the room in an ethereal light. Haley looked like a golden-haired angel curled up in the middle of the king-size bed. Walking over to wake her and ask her why the hell she wasn't in his bed in the master suite, Luke stopped short at the iridescent trace of tears on her flawless cheeks.

She'd been crying?

Without warning the protectiveness he'd experienced at the wedding chapel began to spread throughout his chest and he didn't think twice as he quietly shrugged out of his suit coat and began to loosen his tie and unbutton his shirt. Tossing them on the chair across the room, he removed his shoes and socks, then unzipped his trousers and added them to the growing pile of clothes. Careful not to wake her, Luke pulled back the covers and stretching out on the bed beside her, reached out to take Haley into his arms.

As he pulled her against him, he thought he heard her murmur his name in her sleep, but he didn't have time to dwell on what that might mean when she moved to snuggle against him and placed a delicate hand on his bare chest. The feel of her slender body aligned with his and her soft palm against his hair-roughened flesh sent heat streaking at the speed of light down the length of him and he concentrated on drawing in his next breath.

Suddenly, and completely without warning, the memory of their wedding kiss came rushing back and his body hardened so fast it left him feeling light-headed. The memory of the feel of her perfect lips against his had him wondering what the hell he'd been thinking. Why had he put work ahead of what he knew for certain would have been one of the most exciting nights of his life?

Luke glanced down at Haley's head cradled on his shoulder. He'd like nothing more than to wake her and make love until they both collapsed from exhaustion. But all things considered, he doubted she'd be overly receptive to the idea of sharing her body with the man who had abandoned her in favor of work.

Tightening his arms around her, he forced himself to relax and concentrate on getting some much needed sleep. The first thing in the morning, he'd let her know he regretted the way things had gone the evening before. And once she was in a more congenial mood, they could spend the rest of their stay in the mountains on the plea-surable task of making her pregnant.

* * *

Trying her best to prolong her tantalizing dream, Haley moved closer to the warm, hard masculine body lying next to her. But one by one, as her senses woke up, she became aware of several things at once. The feel of crisp hair beneath her palm, the light woodsy scent of a man's cologne and the sound of soft snores chased away the last traces of sleep and opening her eyes, she found herself face-to-face with Luke.

Her sharp intake of breath must have wakened him because the corners of his mouth slowly curved up in a sleepy smile a moment before he opened his eyes. "Good morning, sweetheart."

"What are you doing here, Luke?"

His low chuckle caused a wonderful fluttering sensation deep in the pit of her stomach and made every one of her feminine instincts come to full alert.

"If you'll remember, we got married yesterday. This is where I'm supposed to be."

"Oh, *I* remember." She shook her head and started moving away from him. She wasn't letting him off the hook that easily. "But I was under the impression that you had forgotten all about that."

The smile on his handsome face faded and before she knew what was happening, he reached out and pulled her back to him. "I really regret that I missed having dinner with you last night." He used his index finger to brush a strand of hair from her cheek. "But during my meeting with the Laurel office staff, I learned about a labor dispute with the work crews which had to be resolved immediately or there would have been a walkout on Monday."

Her skin tingled everywhere he touched her, but Haley tried her best not to notice. As far as she was concerned, no matter what the reason for their marriage, there was no excuse for a man to completely ignore a woman on what was supposed to be one of the most important days of her life.

"There's always going to be something that needs your attention." She tried to wiggle out of his grasp, but his arms were like two steel bands holding her firmly against him.

"That's true," he said, confirming her suspicion that she would always come in a distant second to Garnier Construction. He pressed a kiss to her forehead. "Would you like to know what's going to claim my attention today and tomorrow?"

"Not particularly." She wasn't interested in hearing about labor problems or another meeting with office managers. All she wanted to do was take a shower, get dressed and pack for their return trip.

"That's too bad because I'm going to tell you anyway," he continued as he ran his hand down the outside of her thigh, then back up, bringing the tail of her nightgown to her waist. "Today and tomorrow, you will have my complete and undivided attention."

Haley wasn't sure if her heart skittered to a stop because of what he'd said or from the feel of his hand slipping beneath her gown to caress her lower back. "B-but I thought…I mean, you said we would be going back to Nashville early this morning."

"I've decided that we need time to rectify the situation you brought to my attention the other day at the office. We need to get to know each other on a more…personal level," he said, giving her a smile that warmed her all over and left no doubt about what he had in mind. "We'll head back home in a couple of days."

"Home? Meaning your mansion?"

He nodded as his finger traced the lace edge of her panties. "Didn't you inform the complex that you would be moving? Surely you didn't think you'd be returning to your apartment, did you?"

She shook her head. "I…still have to…move my clothes." How was she supposed to think with his fingers dipping beneath the scalloped trim?

"Don't worry. I had some of my staff move your personal effects after we left yesterday," he stated, his voice low and intimate.

Haley froze. "You did what?"

He kissed her shoulder. "Everything will already be unpacked and put away by the time we get back on Tuesday."

She couldn't believe what she was hearing. "Your arrogance has no bounds, does it?"

"What do you mean?" He had the audacity to look truly puzzled.

"Did it ever occur to you that I might not like someone else handling my underwear?"

He smiled as he continued to touch her and every stroke of his warm palm on her suddenly sensitive skin increased the heat building deep inside of her. "I don't…know what surprises me more…your arrogance or…you taking a day off from work," she explained, struggling to catch her next breath and trying desperately to remember she was irritated with him.

"Why would my taking time off surprise you?" he asked, his warm breath close to her ear.

"The only time I've ever known you to take a day off from the office was when your sister graduated from college," she retorted, trying to concentrate on something besides his hands moving steadily over her body. She was definitely losing the battle.

"I'm not all work," he insisted, slowly easing her to her back. When he leaned over her, his smile and the gleam in his vivid blue eyes told her in no uncertain terms exactly what he meant when he added, "Believe me, I do know how to play, sweetheart."

"I'm, uh, sure you do," she hedged, staring up at him. "But I don't think—"

"That's all right. I'll do the thinking for both of us," he interrupted as he brought his mouth down to cover hers.

His lips teased and caressed, making Haley forget anything she'd been about to say. Wrapping her arms around his broad shoulders, she gave up trying to think and lost herself to his tender exploration.

How could she even begin to form a rational thought when she was lying in bed with a half-naked man? The very man she'd fantasized about for over five years? The man who was kissing her like she was the most desirable woman he'd ever known?

When he used the tip of his tongue to trace the edge of her mouth, she couldn't deny him entry. She wanted to once again experience his taste and the feeling that Luke was claiming her for his own.

Her pulse sped up and she wasn't entirely certain it would ever return to normal when he slowly slid his hand from her back to her abdomen, then up to the underside of her breast. Never in her wildest imaginings could anything have felt more sensual as when he cupped the soft mound and began to relentlessly tease the puckered bud with the pad of his thumb.

"You're so sweet," he said, breaking the kiss to nibble his way down her throat to the top of her nightgown. When he raised his head, he gave her a smile that heated her all the way to her soul at the same time he used his finger to trace the delicate lace edging at the neckline. "Let's get you out of this."

Before she could respond, he tossed the comforter back and propping himself up on one elbow, used both hands to rip the thin cotton garment from the top all the way to the hem.

Gasping, she reached for the sheet. "Good heavens, Luke, you didn't even give me the chance to take it off."

He was not the least bit apologetic when he shoved the sheet farther from her grasp. "I didn't want to waste the time."

"That was the only gown I brought with me…I didn't expect to be staying more than one night," she explained, covering her breasts with her palms.

Taking her hands in his, he moved them to her sides. "Don't try to hide from me, Haley. We're married. There's no reason for you to be embarrassed or shy with me."

"But couldn't we learn about each other on a more personal level with our clothes on first?" she asked as a fiery flush heated her cheeks.

She knew he thought she'd lost her mind, but that couldn't be helped. To have their relationship go from strictly business with no contact outside of the office one day, to being married and naked in bed together the next was more than a little intimidating. And even though she'd dreamed that one day he'd notice her as a woman instead of just his competent assistant, in her fantasies, things between them had never progressed this far this fast.

"I told you before that there's no better way for a man and woman to get acquainted than making love," he reminded, lowering his head to kiss the tip of her breast. "Besides, the sole reason for our getting married was for me to make you pregnant." Laughing, he traced the valley between her breasts all the way down to her navel. "And that would be hard to do with clothes on, sweetheart."

When he lowered his mouth to her overly sensitive nipple, a swirl of heat gathered in the very core of her and Haley forgot about everything but the way Luke was making her feel. Shamelessly threading her fingers through his thick black hair to hold him to her, it took a moment for her to realize he'd slipped his hand below the band of her silk panties.

Inch by slow inch, he caressed his way to her most secret parts, and she thought she'd melt from the delicious heat threading though her veins. The intense longing he created was like nothing she had ever known and she didn't even try to stop her moan from escaping.

"Look at me, Haley," he said, raising his head from her breast. When she did, his smile sent another wave of tingling sensations straight through her. "In the past few minutes, I've already learned several things about you that I wasn't aware of before."

"R-really?"

Smiling, he nodded. "You like the way I make you feel when I touch you here." When he moved his fingers to dip inside and stroke her intimately, every fiber of her being hummed with pleasure.

"I...oh...y-yes."

"And you really like for me to do this," he added, nipping at the tip of her breast with his firm lips.

When he took the bud into his mouth to draw on it deeply, exquisite feelings flowed to every nerve in her body and her will to resist became nonexistent.

Unable to make a sound, she nodded as Luke continued his gentle assault on her senses. Completely lost to the feelings he was creating within her, she didn't have the slightest clue when he'd removed her panties and his boxers. But the feel of his bare body against hers and the solid strength of his arousal as he pressed himself to her thigh, brought back some of her sanity and she shivered from nervous anticipation.

"I've gotten to know you quite well already, sweetheart," Luke informed, kissing her. "But now it's time you learned something about me."

"W-what...would that...be?" she asked, finding oxygen in extremely short supply.

"I want you," he said, nudging her legs apart with his knee. "I want to be deep inside of you. Right now."

As he moved to cover her, she closed her eyes and lay back against the pillows. The electrifying excitement he'd built inside her was undeniable, but so was a fair amount of nervous apprehension.

He'd said that making love was a good way to get to know each other on a more personal level. And there was something very important that he was about to find out about her. Something that she was fairly certain he would have never guessed.

What was Luke going to think when he found out? How was he going to react when he discovered that his wife had never been acquainted with any other man the way she was about to become acquainted with him?

Five

Luke felt Haley's body tense as he guided himself to her and his protectiveness returned tenfold. "Open your eyes, sweetheart." When she did, he thought he saw a brief shadow of fear in her blue-green gaze. "You do trust me, don't you?"

She stared at him a moment before she slowly nodded. "Y-yes. But there's something I should probably tell you."

"Do you want me, Haley?"

"Y-yes."

"That's all I need to know." Giving her what he hoped was a reassuring smile, he brushed her soft lips with his, cutting off anything she was about to say. "It's going to be all right, Haley. I know you haven't been seeing anyone and it's probably been a while. But I don't want you to worry. We're going to be good together and I promise to take care of you." He moved his lower body forward a fraction of an inch. "I'll make sure that you get as much pleasure from our lovemaking as I do, sweetheart."

As he entered her, Luke gritted his back teeth and forced himself to go slow in order to allow her body to adjust to the invasion of his. He'd been right in his assumption that she didn't have a lot of experience at making love. She'd been too inhibited about him seeing her body and he could tell that she'd been genuinely surprised by the way he'd made her feel when he'd touched her. And if that hadn't been evidence enough to prove his theory, the mind-blowing tightness surrounding him now was.

But when he met a slight resistance within her, then the feeling that he'd pushed past a thin barrier, he froze and tried to come to grips with his newest discovery about her. He'd thought it had been some time since she'd been intimate with a man, but it had not even crossed his mind that Haley might still be a virgin. After all, she was twenty-eight years old and extremely attractive. He couldn't believe some man hadn't swept her off her feet at least once.

"You've never had sex." He hadn't meant for the words to come out more as an accusation than a statement of the fact.

"No," she whispered. A couple of tears slipped from the corners of her tightly closed eyes and Luke felt like the biggest fool alive.

He knew she was experiencing a bit of discomfort and careful to hold his lower body completely still, he wrapped his arms around her and cradled her to him. "It's okay, sweetheart. I know it must be uncomfortable, but try to relax. Just a little more and you'll have all of me."

He waited until he felt a slight easing of her feminine muscles surrounding him, then moving forward, joined their bodies completely. The realization that he was claiming her in a way that no other man had, caused the possessiveness within him to reach heights that he never expected and didn't even want to think about.

But concentrating on more pressing matters, he ignored the fire in his belly that urged him to complete the act of loving her. Her body needed more time to get used to the newness of accommodating his. And the very last thing he intended to do was hurt her any more than he had already done.

"It's a little better now," she said, opening her eyes. The spark of desire he detected in the turquoise depths and the easing of tension in her slender form reinforced her statement and he knew that the unfulfilled passion he'd created within her was beginning to return.

As he eased his hips back, he captured her gaze with his. "I want you to promise me that you'll let me know if I'm hurting you in any way."

"I promise," she repeated, bringing her arms up to encircle his shoulders.

The feel of her arms embracing him and her soft body accepting him almost sent him over the edge. But focusing all of his attention on making things as easy for her as was humanly possible, he slowly began to rock against her.

His body demanded satisfaction, but Luke refused to give in to his own needs without ensuring that he'd first met hers. He knew it wasn't always enjoyable for a woman the first time she made love, but even if it killed him, he was going to see that Haley found their love-making at the very least pleasant and if he had his way, quite pleasurable.

When her body began a tentative movement that joined the rhythm of his, he knew his efforts had been worth the hell he'd been going through to ensure her comfort. But all too soon he felt her gently tighten around him, signaling that she'd reached the pinnacle and was about to find the ecstasy he was determined to give her. Deepening his movements, he waited until he felt the trembling of her delicate body beneath his and heard her softly cry out his name before he let go of the slender thread he held on his control. Only then did he give way to his own desire and allow himself to find the release he so desperately needed.

Luke's pulse pounded in his ears and he thought he just might pass out from the rush as he thrust into her one final time and wave after wave of intense pleasure flowed through him. As he filled her with his essence, he felt as if he'd been completely drained of energy and eased himself down on top of her.

He wasn't certain how long he lay covering her as he tried to catch his breath, but when he finally gained enough strength, he moved to her side and gathered her to him. "Are you all right?"

"That was…" She paused as if trying to find the right word. "…absolutely amazing."

Smiling at the fact that he'd taken her virginity and still managed to bring her pleasure, he reached down to pull the sheet over their rapidly cooling bodies. "I promise next time our lovemaking will reach incredible status."

"Really?" She shook her head. "I don't see how it could be any better than what I just experienced."

"That's because you haven't had anything to compare it to." He hugged her close and tried not to dwell on the possessiveness that threatened to consume him. "My mission is to see that every time we make love the pleasure keeps getting stronger for you."

"I'll have to take your word for that," she conceded, sounding extremely sleepy.

He kissed the top of her head pillowed on his shoulder. "Get some rest, sweetheart. We'll talk after you've had a little nap."

As he held Haley while she slept, Luke couldn't quite wrap his mind around the fact that he was the only man to make love to her. Had he ever been a woman's first time before?

If he had, he knew for certain he would have remembered it. Taking a woman's virginity wasn't something a man was likely to forget.

Glancing at Haley sleeping so peacefully next to him, several questions kept running through his mind. Why had she waited so long to be with a man? If she'd been holding out for the permanence of marriage before taking that step, why had she agreed to birth his heir when she knew their arrangement would eventually end? And how had she managed to save herself from players like Chet Parker, who were out there just looking for the right opportunity to swoop in and seduce a woman as beautiful and innocent as Haley?

When Haley moved closer to him in her sleep, he tightened his arms around her and kissed her soft cheek. He didn't want to analyze his uncharacteristic protectiveness toward her or the unfamiliar need to possess her. They'd reached an agreement and she was his for now—the woman he'd chosen to be the mother of his child. As far as he was concerned, that was reason enough.

Oh, he still wanted answers to his questions regarding her lack of sexual experience and an explanation of her motives for agreeing to have his child. But he wasn't overly concerned about getting them right away. As he got to know her better, he'd learn her secrets and reach a satisfactory conclusion to the mystery of Haley Rollins.

In the meantime, he had every intention of enjoying the pleasure of making love to her every night and reaching his goal of soon having an heir to inherit the vast holdings of Garnier Construction.

Slowly opening her eyes, Haley found herself alone in the big log bed and wondered if she'd been dreaming. After all this time imagining what it would be like, had she really slept with Luke?

As she stretched to loosen the kinks of sleep from her limbs, the feel of the sheet sliding over her bare skin and the interesting little aches in her lower body quickly told her that they had indeed consummated their marriage. Her cheeks heated as the memory of what they'd shared in the early predawn light came flooding back.

Luke had seen her as no other man had and made her feel things she would have never thought possible. But once he'd learned she was a virgin, his incredible patience and the extra care he took to reduce any discomfort she might have had touched her deeply. He'd seen to it that her first experience making love was pleasurable and even though their marriage was destined to end one day, she'd never be sorry that she'd waited for her husband.

"I see you finally woke up, sleepyhead," Luke greeted her cheerfully, shouldering the door open. He carried a breakfast tray with two plates of delicious-looking food, glasses of orange juice and a single rose in a glass bud vase. "Time to rise and shine."

His thoughtfulness was unexpected and quite touching. "I haven't had breakfast in bed since I was child," she reminisced, holding the sheet to cover her breasts as she sat up. "And I was too sick to care about eating anything then."

"Well, I hope you have a hearty appetite now, because Mrs. Beck outdid herself," he noted, referring to the housekeeper. "I think she cooked every breakfast food known to man."

"Could you get my overnight case, please?" Haley requested, wanting to retrieve the new bathrobe she'd purchased for the trip.

"Uh-oh." He gave her a sheepish grin. "When I got up and went to shower and change, I moved it to my room."

"What am I going to put on?" she asked, looking around for something—anything—to wear.

"I really like what you're wearing now," he observed, setting the tray on top of the dresser.

"I'm naked under here."

"Bingo."

Her cheeks heated at his lascivious grin. "Seriously, what am I going to wear?"

"I think you wear *nothing* very well," he commented, rocking back on his heels. "It really looks good on you."

"Will you be serious?" she pleaded, feeling a little desperate. "I can't even go downstairs to get my clothes without something to cover up with. Poor Mrs. Beck would probably have a massive coronary."

He looked thoughtful. "I guess you might have a point."

"I do have a point." She shook her head. "And unless you intend for me to stay in this bed the rest of the day, I need something to put on."

"Staying in bed presents some very interesting possibilities," he responded, his grin widening. When she tugged the sheet free from the end of the mattress, he pulled the tail of his shirt from his jeans. "If you're that adamant about it, I'll have to make the sacrifice."

She stared shamelessly as Luke unbuttoned the garment and revealed his wide chest. Earlier when they'd made love, she'd been too nervous and preoccupied with the newness of it all to pay a lot of attention to his physique. But as he shrugged out of the shirt, her breath caught and her heart did a funny little thump against her rib cage.

His body was absolutely perfect. Every muscle from his shoulders all the way to the waistband of his low-slung jeans was well-defined and he was most definitely the type of man dreams were made of. At least, her dreams.

When he handed her the shirt, then stood there expectantly, she forced her thoughts back to the matter at hand and shook her head. "Turn around."

His smile sent a wave of sizzling warmth shimmering over her skin. "Sweetheart, I saw your body when we made love and believe me, you have no reason to be self-conscious. You're beautiful."

"I'll have to take your word on that," she remarked, refusing to give too much weight to his appreciation of her body. "But it's extremely difficult to throw caution to the wind after twenty-eight years of keeping myself covered up."

Apparently deciding she meant business, he finally blew out an exaggerated breath, shook his head and turned his back to her. "We've already made love once and I anticipate doing so again quite frequently. It won't take long before I know your body as well as I know mine."

"In less than a week, we've gone from nothing more than boss and employee to sleeping together," she tried to explain, pulling on his shirt. The delicious masculine scent surrounding her as she buttoned the garment caused Haley to feel warm all over. "We only went on one date—if you want to call it that—and that was the night before we got married."

When he picked up the breakfast tray from the dresser and turned to face her, his expression was thoughtful. "So what you're saying is, you don't switch gears quite that fast."

"Something like that." Maybe he was beginning to understand how she felt.

"I guess that makes sense," he said absently as he set the tray over her lap, then lowered himself to sit on the mattress beside her. He looked pensive for a moment. "Since we're discussing your inhibitions, were they the reason you were still a virgin?"

She knew he'd be curious and ask about it. "It's quite simple, really. I went to a very strict, private high school for girls. In our Freshman year, we were encouraged to take a pledge to stay pure until we married. I promised that I would." Reaching for a slice of crispy bacon, she shrugged. "Besides, I never met a man that I cared enough about to be intimate with."

"Never?"

"Oh, I was tempted a couple of times in college with one or two of the guys I dated." She shook her head. "But I always found a reason not to break my vow. Probably because it just didn't feel right with them."

"Do you always keep your word, Haley?" His question was casual enough, but she could tell he was extremely interested in her answer.

Swallowing the bacon she'd been nibbling on, she nodded. "It's not always easy, but if I tell someone that I'll do something, I try my best to do it." She smiled. "I have had to break my promises a few times, but I've never made a habit of it."

"So that's why you followed through when I called your bluff about having to be married," he proclaimed, capturing her gaze with his. "You gave me your word."

Haley nodded again. She wasn't overly surprised that he'd figured out that she was discouraging him when she laid down the terms to have his baby. He was very perceptive and it was one of the many reasons he was such a highly successful businessman.

"Knowing how you feel about relationships, I thought mentioning marriage would dissuade you," she admitted. "If I'd tried to back out when you said you were agreeable, you wouldn't have given me a minute's peace until I honored my word."

"That's true, but why didn't you just reject my request outright?" he asked, obviously trying to figure out what made her tick as he took a big bite of his scrambled eggs.

"Because I know you well enough that when you set your sights on something, you don't give up. You're like a dog with a juicy bone." Picking up her glass of orange juice, she gazed at him over the rim. "Would you have abandoned the idea of me having your child if I'd said no right away?"

Chuckling, he shook his head. "Not a chance in hell, sweetheart."

"My point exactly."

"So, if you know me so well," he argued as he placed his fork on his empty plate, "why do you keep insisting that we need to get to know each other further?"

How could she explain that it was the little everyday things that she wanted to know?

"Do you have any idea why my hair is straight when I'm at the office, but when I'm at home it's curly?" she finally asked.

His expression clearly stated he thought she'd lost her mind.

"Bear with me for a minute."

He gave her a dubious look. "Okay. I assume you're like my sister and use a curling iron when you want to make your hair curly."

"Just the opposite." She couldn't help but laugh. "I use a flat iron to take the curl *out*."

"Your hair is naturally curly?" He shook his head. "I wasn't aware of that."

"That's what I meant about knowing each other. Don't you think that's something a man would know about the woman he has a child with?"

He looked thoughtful. "I suppose it might be since it's a trait that could be passed on to my son." Grinning, he winked at her. "But it's certainly not a requirement for having sex."

Luke wasn't going to concede easily. But neither was she.

"I know how you take your coffee. Do you know how I prefer mine?"

He was silent for several seconds before he finally answered. "No."

"That's something else most couples know about each other by the time they walk down the aisle or have a baby." She smiled. "And just for the record, I don't drink coffee because I don't like the taste of it."

"I never noticed," he acknowledged as he picked up the tray. "But I think I have an excellent way of remedying this little problem you think we have while learning each others' likes and dislikes."

"Really? What would that be?"

"We're going to take a drive across the mountains over into North Carolina. And while we're traveling, we'll take turns asking questions about the little everyday things." He looked quite pleased with himself. "It won't take any time at all and we'll know each other quite well."

"But I thought you had plans to stay here for the rest of the weekend," she reminded him, fascinated by the play of muscles in his broad back as he balanced the tray and walked to the door.

Stopping, he turned. "That was before I took your virginity."

"What does that have to do with anything?" she asked, getting out of bed to find her clothes and take a shower.

Luke suddenly groaned, closed his eyes and drew in a deep breath.

Alarmed by his uncharacteristic behavior, she went to him. "Are you all right?"

When he opened his eyes, the intensity in his incredible blue gaze warmed her. "Do you have any idea how sexy you look wearing nothing but my shirt? Or what a turn-on it is for me just knowing that you don't have anything on underneath it?"

"Not really." She wondered if he knew how sexy he looked *without* a shirt.

"The reason we need to go for a drive is because if we don't, I'm going to put down this tray, carry you back to bed and make love to you until we both collapse from exhaustion." He glanced away. "And that wouldn't be a good idea right now."

Had he changed his mind about wanting her to become pregnant immediately?

"Why not? Isn't that a prerequisite for making a baby the old-fashioned way?"

"Sweetheart, nothing would make me happier than making love to you all day and all night." He gazed at her and shook his head. "But you're new to this and I'm sure you're a little sore. If we wait until this evening, it might not be as uncomfortable for you as it would be now."

Haley felt as if her cheeks were on fire. She wasn't used to discussing something so intimate and personal. "Oh, I...um, didn't realize."

"We'll make love again tonight." He gave her a quick kiss, then walked out into the hall. "Now, do me a favor. Go down to the master suite and get ready. We'll leave as soon as the rental car agency can have a car delivered."

When she started to walk past him, he shook his head.

"Let me go first."

"Why?"

Giving her a look so sensual it could have easily turned a stone to mush, he started down the hall. "Because if you walk downstairs ahead of me, I'll end up hard as hell. And when I take the tray back to the kitchen, I don't think Mrs. Beck could stand the shock of seeing me in that condition."

"That might even traumatize her more than me wearing nothing but a sheet," she said, laughing.

Luke snorted. "Knowing Mrs. Beck, I'd put money on it."

As Haley followed him toward the stairs, a tiny feminine thrill flowed through her at the knowledge that he was that attracted to her. She wasn't foolish enough to think that just because he wanted her, that he cared deeply for her. But if he desired her now, maybe one day he would develop true feelings for her.

As Luke steered the rental car into a parking area at Chimney Rock in North Carolina, Haley gazed at the lush green mountains surrounding the natural monolith. "I see why this location was chosen for several movies. It's absolutely gorgeous. Can you imagine how fantastic the hiking must be around here?"

Turning off the car's engine, he smiled. "Did I just learn another little known fact about you that I wouldn't have guessed? Are you a hiker?"

"Not anymore." She looked out at the panoramic view. "But I used to go hiking all the time when I was younger."

"Let me guess. One of the college boyfriends appreciated nature."

"Not hardly. They might have gotten their hands dirty." Just the thought of any of them going anywhere that took them outside of a climate-controlled environment was laughable. "My passion for hiking started long before college. I went on nature walks when I joined the Campfire Girls. Then later, when I was in high school, I joined the hiking club."

"Interesting."

"What about you? Do you enjoy any outdoor activities?" She grinned. "Surveying the work-in-progress at a job site doesn't count."

He laughed. "But that's outdoors and I do enjoy watching another Garnier project take shape."

She shook her head. "That's something I already know about you. Remember, we're supposed to be sharing the unknown."

"Right. Let's see, Jake and I used to go on an annual camping trip in the Sierras," he replied, referring to his twin brother. "But in the past several years, we've both been so busy that we haven't had time."

"Did you enjoy those trips to the mountains?" she asked, trying to imagine what it would be like to have a family to share things with.

Looking thoughtful for several seconds, he nodded. "We'd spend an entire week fishing and catching up on what plans we were making to advance our careers."

"You should make the time to do that again, Luke." If she had a brother or sister, nothing would stand in the way of their spending time together. "You know what they say about taking the time to smell the roses."

"I'll keep that in mind," he indicated, getting out of the car to come around and open the passenger door for her. "What about you, do you have a family tradition with one of your siblings?"

Taking the hand he offered to help her out of the car, she tried not to meet his questioning gaze. If she did, he might see how truly alone and sad she'd always felt.

"I was an only child," she revealed.

"Really?" Closing the car door, he put his arm around her waist and tucked her to his side as they walked to the edge of the scenic overlook. "I wasn't aware of that."

Before he could question her further about her family, she pointed to a black bear and two small cubs that waddled into a clearing on the slope below. "Aren't they adorable?"

He snorted. "I suppose, if you like a lot of fur and really big teeth."

"I love babies of all kinds," she confirmed as she watched the two cubs engage in an impromptu wrestling match.

"What about alligator babies?" Turning her to face him, he pulled her close. "They don't have fur, but they do have a lot of teeth. You don't think they're cute, do you?"

The feel of his arms around her sent a languid heat flowing through every part of her. "Well, they may not be as sweet as a live teddy bear, but I'm sure the momma alligator thinks they are."

He stared at her for several long moments, then slowly lowered his head to capture her lips in a kiss so tender it brought tears to her eyes. Thoughtful and sweet, Luke explored her with a thoroughness that made her feel as if he truly cherished everything about her.

But when he slipped his tongue inside her mouth to taste and tease, the kiss became so steamy that Haley felt as if the earth moved beneath her feet. Stroking her inner recesses at the same time he pressed his hips against her belly caused an empty ache to settle deep in the most feminine areas of her body. The feel of his strong arousal and the mastery of his kiss caused her knees to give way and she clung to his solid strength for support.

"I think we'd better head back. Otherwise, I'm going to abandon my good intentions and make love to you right here and now," he vowed, breaking the kiss. "Besides, there's one other place I think you'd enjoy seeing."

"Really? Where would that be?" she questioned, not really caring as long as they were together.

"You'll see," he promised, guiding her to the car.

Two and a half hours later, as they stepped onto the moving walkway that led through the acrylic tunnel at the aquarium in Gatlinburg, they were immediately surrounded by thousands of species of aquatic creatures. "This is wonderful, Luke," Haley declared, marveling at the activity surrounding them. "It's like being underwater."

"You find this interesting, do you?"

"Absolutely." She smiled at a couple of orange and white striped fish gliding effortlessly through the water. "Aren't they sweet?"

Luke snorted. "I've never associated that word with fish." He smiled suddenly. "Let me guess, you're thinking of the cartoon movie that came out several years ago about a lost clown fish."

"You know about that?" she asked, somewhat surprised. She wouldn't have thought he'd have known anything about a children's movie.

Nodding, he shrugged. "Arielle insisted that Jake and I had to take her to see it when it first came out. It was part of her birthday present and we couldn't get out of it."

"Did you enjoy it?"

"I suppose it was a good kid movie," he commented, gazing at a shark lazily gliding toward them. "But I normally prefer psychological thrillers or action/adventure movies."

"Not the best for a growing child." She paused, then glancing at him from the corner of her eye to make sure she had his attention, she went on. "You do realize that you'll be taking in a lot of cartoon films once the baby gets old enough to enjoy them."

He frowned and it was obvious that he hadn't thought past grooming his heir to take over his business holdings once the child was old enough. "Why don't I leave that part of the parenting to you?" he finally suggested.

"Why don't we do that part together?" she shot back. "Don't you think a child would like to go a few places and do a few things with both parents at the same time? It would be nice for our child to know her parents are on good terms. And you do want the baby to grow up to be happy and well-adjusted, don't you?"

"Of course, but I hadn't really given activities and the like a lot of thought." He was silent for a moment as if digesting what she'd said. "But it probably would be a good idea for us to do things together with him."

Satisfied that she had Luke contemplating the emotional needs of a growing child, she decided to give him one more thing to think about. "You know that the baby could turn out to be a girl."

He looked thoughtful. "Something else I hadn't considered. I just assumed my heir would be a son."

"Would it make a difference if we had a daughter?" she asked, needing to know how he would react if she had a girl.

"No. I've met several women with excellent business instincts. You included." As they stepped off the moving walkway, he turned to face her and the expression on his face caused heat to shimmer over every inch of her. "You're going to be a wonderful mother, Haley, and not just for the traits I want passed on to our child."

"You really think so?"

He nodded. "Now, what do you say we head back to the lodge? I think it's time we stopped talking about the baby and get started making one."

Several hours later, standing on the balcony staring out at the night sky, Luke watched a shooting star disappear behind Mount LeConte as he thought about the day's events. He'd had one of the most fascinating, and at the same time, frustrating afternoons of his life. And Haley was completely responsible.

On one hand, he'd been intrigued by the things he'd learned about her. He now knew that her favorite color was lavender, that she couldn't resist anything chocolate and that she had a weakness for babies, whether they were human, animal or fish.

He smiled at the thought of her reaction to the mother

black bear and two chubby little cubs they'd observed when they stopped at Chimney Rock. Her excitement and joy at seeing the baby animals at play had sparkled in her turquoise eyes and been reflected in her soft laughter. And he couldn't get over how happy he'd been to share the moment with her. She was going to be a wonderful mother and he was convinced now more than ever that he'd made the right choice for the mother of his heir.

But on the other hand, the day had been sheer hell. He'd noticed things about her that he'd never paid attention to before—how sweet and feminine her voice sounded, how pretty she was when she smiled and how graceful and sensual every move of her body was when they got out of the car at the scenic overlook and when they'd strolled through the aquarium.

He'd spent every minute they were together in a perpetual state of arousal. All he'd been able to think about was getting back to the lodge, taking their clothes off and making love to her the entire night.

And that was what really had him perplexed. After making love to her, he'd started thinking less about having sex for the purpose of making her pregnant and more about giving her immeasurable pleasure. In fact, she'd been the one to remind him about having the baby and how they should share the responsibility of raising the child.

"Mrs. Beck and I finished cleaning up the kitchen," Haley said, walking out onto the deck. "She said to tell you she's leaving and will be back tomorrow morning in time to prepare breakfast."

At the sound of her voice, Luke glanced over his shoulder. She looked amazingly beautiful in her yellow blouse and khaki slacks, but he liked the way she'd looked in his shirt a hell of a lot better. Or better yet, out of it.

The thought caused his body to tighten predictably and he forced himself to remember what she'd just said. "You didn't have to help Mrs. Beck. That's what I pay the woman for."

"I'm used to it," she advised, walking over to stand next to him. "Even before I moved out on my own, I sometimes helped my father's housekeeper with the cooking and cleaning."

It was her first mention of anything about her family. "I take it your folks are fairly well off?"

Earlier in the day, he wondered why she deflected the sibling talk. She had at least met his siblings the few times they'd stopped by his office and knew that after their mother's death, he and Jake had raised their younger sister. But he knew absolutely nothing about her family, beyond her telling him that she was an only child.

"My father wasn't overly wealthy, but he did all right," she finally stated, shrugging.

"And your mother?"

"Was completely out of the picture." He watched her cross her arms beneath her breasts and fix her gaze on the mountains.

Haley's defensive body language and the sadness he detected in her voice surprised him. "We don't have to talk about it, sweetheart," he ventured, reaching for her.

When he took her into his arms and held her close, Luke wondered what had happened to her mother. But remembering the look on her pretty face when she'd asked him at the aquarium if it would matter if his heir was a girl made him wonder about the relationship she shared with her father, as well. But his curiosity could wait. She clearly didn't want to discuss any of that now.

He could respect that. The anger and resentment caused by an absentee parent was certainly familiar ground for him. Besides, he had no intention of spoiling what had, up until that moment, been a damned good day.

"Why don't we get in the hot tub and relax for a while before we go to bed for the night?" he asked, nuzzling her soft curls.

"I can't." She sounded less than certain as she brought her arms up to his shoulders. "I didn't bring my swimsuit."

Nibbling on her earlobe, he smiled when he felt a tremor course through her. "We don't have to wear suits. In fact, I think it would be a lot more fun to go skinny-dipping."

"I—I don't think so."

Her breathy laughter sent a shaft of heat straight to the region south of his belt buckle.

"If I couldn't drop the sheet in front of you this morning, what makes you think I could go skinny-dipping with you in the hot tub this evening?"

"Well, for one thing it's dark and we're alone on this section of the mountain." He trailed kisses down the column of her neck. When she sagged against him, he added, "And for another, I promise I won't peek until you're settled in the water."

"Why am I having trouble believing that?" Her throaty question sent his blood pressure soaring.

He chuckled. "How did you know I used up all of my allocated honor for the day?"

"Just a lucky guess."

When she threaded her fingers in the hair at the nape of his neck the heat in his lower belly turned into a hungry flame.

"I suppose we could wear our underwear in the hot tub," she suggested.

His internal heat flared out of control and threatened to turn him to a cinder when she kissed the exposed skin at the open collar of his shirt. "I've got an even better idea, sweetheart," he revealed as he swung her up into his arms. He carried her through the French doors of the great room and straight to the master suite. "Why don't we skip the hot tub and just go to bed?"

Six

As Luke cradled her to him, Haley put her arms around his shoulders and allowed him to carry her to his bedroom. They'd spent a wonderful day together with moments that she would never forget. And if she hadn't been sure she loved him before, Haley knew for certain that she did now.

When he set her on her feet at the side of his bed, then reached over to switch on the bedside lamp, Haley's heart thumped so hard against her ribs she was truly surprised it wasn't deafening. She hadn't anticipated they would be undressing in front of each other or that the light would be on when they did. But it appeared that was exactly what Luke had in mind as he bent to remove both of their shoes and socks. Straightening, he pulled her back into his arms.

"If we'd gotten in the hot tub without our clothes on, you were going to peek, weren't you?" she asked.

Grinning, he nodded. "Shamelessly, sweetheart."

"I think I probably would have, too," she admitted.

"I assume this means that after today you feel we've reached a more personal level and you're more comfortable with me?" he commented, sliding his hands from her back down to the curve of her hips.

"I know you think I've been ridiculous about our knowing more about each other. But you only knew Haley Rollins, the executive assistant who runs your office." She raised her gaze to meet his. "I wanted you to learn about Haley Rollins, the woman."

His gaze was positively sizzling as Luke studied her before he slowly began to lower his head. "And I'm glad I got to know the real Haley. You're warm, compassionate and…" He brushed her lips with his. "…so damned sexy I can't keep my hands off you."

When his mouth covered hers, Haley's eyes drifted shut and her heart soared. Maybe there was hope. Maybe in time Luke could learn to care for her as deeply as she loved him.

But as his firm lips explored her with a tenderness that robbed her of breath, she lost herself in his kiss and abandoned all speculation of what the future might hold for them. All that mattered was she was in his arms now and it felt absolutely wonderful.

As he coaxed her to open for him, she didn't think twice about parting her lips and granting him access. She wanted to once again experience the mastery of his kiss and taste his growing need for her.

Tentatively touching her tongue to his, a tingling excitement filled every cell of her being and she felt as if her insides had been turned to soft, warm butter. Wrapping her arms around his trim waist, her heart raced and the delicious warmth spread inside her as she enjoyed the feel of his hard masculine body pressed so closely to hers.

Slowly easing the pressure of his mouth on hers, he broke the kiss and leaned back to capture her gaze with his. "Why don't we get a little more comfortable?" he suggested, reaching to release the button at the top of her blouse. His slow, promising smile sent shivers coursing throughout her body. "Do you have any idea how much I'm going to enjoy taking these clothes off you?"

"I really…hadn't given it…a lot of thought," she said breathlessly. His fingers grazing her breasts as he unfastened the next button made it seem as if the air had suddenly been sucked right out of the room.

"Have you given any thought to what it would be like taking my clothes off?"

Every night in her fantasies for the past five years, but she wasn't about to admit that to him. "I'm certainly thinking a lot about it now."

By the time he finished with the buttons on her blouse, then slid the silk fabric from her shoulders and down her arms, Haley wondered if she'd ever draw another breath. The feel of his hands skimming over her skin as he whisked the top from her body was absolute heaven. She wanted his touch, wanted to again feel the same delicious sensations he'd created within her that morning. But just when she thought he would remove her bra and touch her the way he had when they made love, he surprised her.

"Let's make this a little more equal, sweetheart," he offered, taking her hands in his to guide them to the front of his shirt.

She knew what he was doing and she loved him all the more for it. Luke wasn't only making an attempt to help her feel more comfortable by allowing her the freedom of undressing him, he was encouraging her to do a little exploring of her own.

As she worked the first button free, she kissed the warm, tanned skin just below his collarbone. "I think I'm really going to like this."

"And I think it's going to kill me," he muttered, sounding more than a little winded.

"You don't like what I'm doing?" she asked as she pushed another button free. She kissed the exposed area, then glancing up at him, kissed her way to the next button. "Would you like for me to stop?"

"Not on…your life." He paused as if trying to arrange his thoughts. "Don't get me wrong, sweetheart. What you're doing feels damned good." When she released the next two buttons and nibbled all the way down his chest to the rippling muscles of his abdomen, she was thrilled at the sound of his sharp intake of breath and the shuddering of his body. "But if you go much farther, I'm going to be finished way before we ever get started."

"Hmm, I don't think that would be good," she confessed, smiling as she pulled the tail of his shirt from the waistband of his low slung jeans.

Laughing, he shook his head. "No, it wouldn't be good at all." Looking up at him, Luke's eyes were tightly closed and a muscle along his jaw was working overtime. "Are you feeling all right?" she asked, thrilled that he seemed to be enjoying her efforts to arouse him.

"I will be real soon," he answered.

When he opened his eyes, the intense blaze of passion in the dark blue depths heated her all the way to her feminine core.

His gaze held her captive as he slowly shrugged out of his shirt, then reached behind her to make quick work of unfastening her lacy bra. When he slid the straps down her arms and tossed it at their feet, he took her hands in his and stood back to gaze at her.

"You're absolutely beautiful, Haley. I don't ever want you to doubt that."

He must have expected her to cover herself because before she had an opportunity to react, he pulled her to him. At the initial feel of soft, feminine skin meeting hard, masculine flesh, the fluttering in her stomach went completely berserk and tiny electric charges skipped over every nerve ending in her body. The delightful abrasion of his chest hair against her sensitized nipples was so sensual, so incredibly exciting, Haley never wanted it to end. And apparently the sensations were just as intense for him as they were for her.

A groan rumbled up from deep in his chest and he took a deep breath a moment before he shook his head. "This was a mistake," he said, splaying his hands over her bare back to hold her to him.

"W-why do you say that?" She was truly surprised that her vocal cords still worked, let alone that she had the capability of putting words into a coherent thought.

Sliding his hands from her back down to her hips, he cupped her bottom and pulled her more fully into the cradle of his hips. The solid ridge of his arousal pressed to her lower stomach threatened to send her into a total meltdown and she had to force herself to breathe.

"You've made me harder than a chunk of granite." Holding her to him with one arm, he reached for the waistband of her khaki slacks. "I want you so damned much I'm about to explode."

As spirals of heat twined their way throughout her body to gather in an ever-tightening coil at the apex of her thighs, Haley couldn't speak. Weakened by the urgent desire building inside of her, she grasped Luke's biceps to stay on her feet.

"You feel so good," he said as his lips moved over her collarbone, then down the slope of her breast.

As he unfastened the closure at the top of her slacks and lowered the zipper, she unbuckled his belt and released the snap of his jeans. Then, feeling bolder than ever, she toyed with the tab at his fly a moment before slowly easing it downward a fraction of an inch.

"I thought we were supposed to be…" Her heart skipped several beats when her fingers brushed the insistent bulge straining to be released from the denim fabric. "…taking each other's clothes off."

When he shuddered and caught her hands in his, their eyes met and the hunger she saw in the navy blue depths sent a shiver of anticipation skipping over her. "Haley, before this night is over, I fully intend for you to know every inch of my body, as I'm going to know every inch of yours," he said, his voice sounding deeper and sexier than she'd ever heard it.

As she watched, he finished lowering his fly, shoved his jeans and boxers down his long muscular legs, then stepped out of them and kicked them to the side. When he straightened, he stood proudly in front of her and she knew he was giving her the luxury of perusing his body without the hindrance of feeling self-conscious about her own.

With her stomach fluttering like a swarm of butterflies had been trapped inside, her gaze slowly slid from his muscular midsection down to his lean, well-toned hips, then beyond. Her breath caught in her throat and her pulse pounded in her ears at the sight of his proud, heavily aroused sex surrounded by a thick patch of crisp dark hair.

"Oh heavens," she said, her gaze flying up to meet his.

As he wrapped his arms around her and drew her to him, his smile made her feel as if she were the most desired woman alive. "I give you my word that making love this time will be easier, sweetheart," he promised as he slid his hands to her waist. "I'm going to give you nothing but pure pleasure."

Unable to find words adequate enough to express how she felt, Haley simply nodded and waited for him to lower the last barriers between them.

"Do you have any idea the hell I've gone through today just knowing what your clothes have been hiding?" he asked, when he added her slacks and panties to the pile of clothing beside them.

"I-I didn't…realize—"

"Let's get into bed while we've still got enough strength left to get there," he cautioned, his words vibrating against her lips.

"That's probably…a good idea," she agreed, trying to catch her non-existent breath.

The world suddenly tilted precariously when he

lifted her in his arms to gently place her in the middle of his bed. As he stretched out beside her, she briefly wondered if he was thinking about making love to her or if he was concentrating on making her pregnant. But as he pulled her to him and she saw the raw hunger in the vivid blue depths of his eyes, she forgot about the purpose behind their union and concentrated on the way he was making her feel.

As he kissed her with a tenderness that robbed her of patience, heat streaked from every part of her to gather in a pool in her very core and she briefly wondered if she'd ever breathe again. But when he cupped her breasts and chafed the overly sensitive tip with the pad of his thumb, a shiver rippled the length of her spine and she moaned from the pure pleasure of it.

"Does that feel good, Haley?" he asked as he nibbled tiny kisses to the rapidly fluttering pulse at the base of her throat.

"Y-yes."

He slid his hand over her ribs to her waist. Then, as he kissed his way from her collarbone down the slope of her breast, he moved his hand to her hip. "Would you like for me to do more?"

"I-If you don't, I think I'll go out of my mind," she groaned, meaning it. She needed his touch, needed his lovemaking like she needed her next heartbeat.

The overwhelming hunger in her lower belly quickly turned to an emptiness that needed to be filled when he took the hardened bud into his mouth and teased her with his tongue at the same time he touched her intimately. Tremors of desire ran through her at the speed of light, but when he slipped his finger inside it felt as if fireworks had been ignited in her soul.

Wanting to bring him the same kind of pleasure, she flattened her palms on his chest and caressed the firm pads of his pectoral muscles, then used her fingertips to trace the lines of his abs on the way to his flat lower belly. But unsure if she should touch him as intimately as he touched her, her hands stilled.

"Go ahead, sweetheart. I promise I won't break," he reassured her, taking her hand in his to guide her to his rigid flesh.

As she encircled his hard masculinity, Haley was encouraged by his deep shuddering groan and she took the liberty of measuring his strength, of teasing his velvety tip and exploring the softness below. But all too quickly Luke took her hands in his and brought them back to his wide chest.

His gaze never left hers as without another word he nudged her knees apart and moved to settle himself between her thighs. "Only pleasure this time," he repeated as he slowly moved his hips forward. "I promise."

Trusting him as she'd never trusted any other man, she didn't even think to be apprehensive. She wanted him to love her, wanted him to take her back to the heights of ecstasy that he'd taken her to that morning.

A shimmering heat began to dance behind Haley's tightly closed eyes when she felt the blunt tip of him against the most feminine part of her. "Please make love to me, Luke. I need you inside. Now."

The blood in her veins felt as if it flowed to the beat of a sultry drum as he slowly began to enter her. Wrapping her arms around his broad shoulders, she reveled in the exquisite stretching of her body as she became one with the man she loved.

When their bodies were completely joined, Haley closed her eyes and lost herself in the intimacy of it all. It felt as if there was no beginning and no end as he set a slow, leisurely pace and wave after wave of pleasure began to consume her. Tension, sensual and exhilarating, began to grip every fiber of her being. Apparently sensing that she was rapidly approaching the peak, Luke deepened his thrusts and she suddenly broke free of the ever-tightening need holding her captive.

Basking in the delicious crescendo of sensations overcoming her, she clung to him to keep from losing herself and held him close in an effort to prolong the feelings. Then suddenly, she felt his body go perfectly still a moment before he hoarsely called her name and joined her in the peace of sweet release.

Haley tightened her arms around Luke and tried not to think about their arrangement being temporary. How long after she became pregnant would he still desire her? Would he view the pregnancy as "mission accomplished" and lose interest in their lovemaking?

And what would happen if she didn't get pregnant right away? Would Luke become impatient and end their arrangement prematurely? Would he decide to find someone else to have the baby both wanted so badly but for different reasons?

She forced herself to end her disturbing speculation as he rolled to her side and drew her to him. All too soon her questions would be answered. Until then, she would store up every memory that she could for the cold, lonely nights when she would be without him.

* * *

Cursing a blue streak, Luke bolted out of bed and hurriedly searched for his jeans in the pile of clothing on the bedroom floor. Who the hell would be calling him at this hour of the night? And why couldn't he find his damned cell phone?

"Do you have any idea what the hell time it is?" he demanded when he finally found his phone and ended its incessant noise.

"I don't give a damn what time it is, we need to talk."

At the sound of his twin brother's voice, Luke growled, "This had better be important, Jake."

"There's something wrong with Arielle," Jake said, unaffected by Luke's harsh tone.

Luke's irritation at being wakened in the middle of the night instantly disappeared at the mention of his younger sister. "Is she all right? What's happened? Does she need a doctor?"

"I'm not sure." Jake paused. "She tells me she's fine, but when I called her this evening she was sobbing her heart out. Again."

"Again? You mean this has happened before? How recently? And why haven't I heard about it until now?" Luke demanded. Normally, he and Jake shared everything. Especially their concerns about their younger sister.

"She begged me not to say anything to you the first time it happened," Jake answered. "And I figured it was just one of those emotional things women do when they have a bad day."

Checking to see if his conversation had disturbed Haley, Luke found her still sleeping peacefully in his bed. Satisfied, he turned his attention to the matter at hand. Normally a very happy person, Arielle rarely cried unless something was terribly wrong.

"How many times has this happened?"

"Twice," Jake confirmed. "And you and I both know this isn't like her."

"Did she tell you why?" Luke inquired, quietly opening the door and walking into the great room.

"I asked, but she wouldn't tell me. And that's what has me concerned. She's never kept anything from us before." Jake's frustration was evident in his tone. "The only thing she would say was we couldn't fix everything for her and that she'd work it out on her own."

That wasn't like their younger sister at all. From the time she could talk, Arielle had shared everything that went on in her life with them and never hesitated to come to either one of them with whatever problem she had.

"Maybe she's having second thoughts about this deal she insisted we all make with Emerald Larson," Luke offered, thinking aloud. God only knew he'd had more than his fair share of misgivings.

"I seriously doubt it." Jake snorted disgustedly. "She told me last week that she's already put in her resignation at the preschool, given notice on her apartment and couldn't wait to move to Dallas."

Luke remained silent as he thought of what could possibly be wrong with their little sister. "Don't women sometimes cry when they go through that hormonal change each month?" he asked, wondering if Haley was prone to mood swings.

"How the hell should I know? If you'll remember, when Arielle went through puberty, we didn't have a clue what to tell her and ended up having our secretaries talk to her about what was going on with her body," Jake huffed, sounding just as clueless as Luke felt. "Since neither one of us has a wife to talk to her, should we have your assistant give her a call and find out what the deal is? They seemed to hit it off pretty well the last couple of times she and I flew into Nashville for a visit."

Luke took a deep breath. He'd intended to call Jake and tell him about his plan for an heir and his agreement with Haley once they returned to Nashville. But since he had his brother on the phone, Luke figured there was no time like the present to fill Jake in.

"Well, you're half right about that statement," he admitted, anticipating his brother's reaction. "You might not be married, but I took the plunge this weekend."

There was a shocked silence before Jake shouted. "You did *what?* And why didn't I hear about this sooner?"

"I didn't make my decision until this past week."

"What the hell were you thinking?" Jake countered, sounding thoroughly disgusted. "Haven't you been listening when I tell you about all the nasty divorce cases I handle?"

Explaining his reasons for wanting a son, Luke carefully omitted Haley's name when he told his brother about the agreement they'd reached. His brother had been teasing him for several years about having hired Haley to add beauty to the Garnier offices. Odd that Jake had noticed years ago what Luke had only recently discovered about her. But then, Jake had always taken an interest in every woman he'd ever laid eyes on.

"Are you sure you can trust this woman?" Jake sounded more than a little doubtful. "How long have you known her?"

"Five years and I have no reason not to trust her," Luke confirmed, realizing that he'd never put his faith in any other woman the way he did Haley. "She's above reproach."

"I wish I had a dollar for every time I've heard that." Always the divorce attorney, Jake demanded "What about a prenup? Please tell me you had her sign one."

"Signed, sealed and airtight," Luke answered.

"You should have had me look it over," Jake groused, clearly disappointed that he'd been excluded from Luke's plan.

"I would have if there had been time," Luke reiterated, meaning it. "But I needed to move on this before she changed her mind."

"So what if she had? I'm sure you could find another one willing to be the surrogate," Jake said reasonably. "And you might not have had to get married to get what you wanted."

Luke shook his head. "I didn't want anyone else. This woman is perfect. She has every trait I'm looking to pass on to my heir."

Several long seconds passed before Jake spoke again. "Well, now that you're out of the running, I guess it won't bother you if I make my move on that sweet little assistant of yours. You know how hot I've always thought she was."

"I have it on good authority that Haley's husband wouldn't appreciate your plan to include her as the object of one of your sexual interludes," Luke grumbled, suddenly more angry with his brother than he could ever remember and not entirely sure why.

He told himself it was because Jake was a notorious player and changed women as often as he changed his socks. But the truth of the matter was, Luke couldn't stand the thought of any other man touching Haley.

Jake was silent before he finally spoke again. "Well, I'll be damned. Haley is my new sister-in-law, isn't she, Luke?"

Still trying to come to grips with the uncharacteristic possessiveness threatening to consume him, Luke ran his hand over the tension building at the back of his neck. "Yeah."

"I wondered how long it would take for you to finally wake up." Jake sounded genuinely surprised. "I'd almost given up on you noticing what a looker she is."

"I told you the sole purpose of the marriage is to have my heir. It's only a temporary thing."

To Luke's immense displeasure, Jake laughed like a damned hyena. "You keep telling yourself that, bro, and you might just start to believe it."

If Luke could have reached through the phone, he'd have cheerfully choked his twin. "Did anyone ever tell you what a smart-ass you are, Jake?"

"You do just about every time we talk," Jake declared, his continued laughter irritating Luke beyond words.

Luke took a deep breath. "We've spent more than enough time talking about me and my current situation. Can we get back to the real reason you woke me up in the middle of the night?"

"I just wanted to give you the heads up about Arielle,"

Jake confirmed, his voice turning serious. "Maybe you can figure out what's wrong the next time the two of you talk."

"I'll give her a call when I get back to Nashville," Luke indicated. "If I find out anything, I'll let you know."

"Okay." His brother paused a moment before adding, "And in the meantime, you tell that sweet little woman of yours that her favorite brother-in-law said 'welcome to the family.'"

"It's temporary, Jake."

"So you say, bro. So you say."

"Shut up."

"Then I don't suppose you'll have a problem with me kissing the bride the next time I see her?"

Luke knew that his brother was baiting him, but it didn't seem to matter. "Try it and die."

At the sound of Jake's hearty laughter, Luke punched the end button and walking back into the bedroom, tossed the cell phone on top of the pile of clothing on the floor. He wasn't sure who he was angrier with—Jake or himself.

In all fairness to Jake, he'd just been his typical devil-may-care self. But Luke, on the other hand, had abandoned his usual reserve and displayed all the self-control of an enraged bull.

What he couldn't understand was why his brother's kidding bothered him so much. And why, when Jake mentioned making a move on Haley and then warned that he was going to "kiss the bride," Luke had been angry enough to bite nails in two.

But as he looked at Haley still sound asleep, he abandoned his speculation. He had a warm, willing woman in his bed and a lot more pleasurable things on his mind than his smart-aleck brother's sense of humor.

Seven

A week after their return to Nashville, Haley gathered a report on one of Garnier's current building projects and walked into Luke's private office. "I've run the numbers on the Robinson build as you requested and it appears that we're going to come in under budget by at least a few hundred thousand dollars, maybe a little more."

"Good to hear," Luke said without looking up from his computer. "Close the door, Haley."

Anticipating a confidential discussion on one of the current Garnier construction projects, she closed the door and sat down in the chair in front of his desk. Since their return to the office, they'd resumed their business-as-usual relationship during the day. Luke was still the no-nonsense, workaholic boss he'd always been and she was the executive assistant he relied on to keep his office running smoothly. To the outward eye, everything was just as it had always been, no single thing had changed. They even drove to the Garnier office in separate cars.

But at home it was an entirely different story. When they were alone in his mansion, Luke was warm, compassionate and an absolutely insatiable lover. And she was the object of his attention from the moment they closed the door until they walked back out the next morning for work.

Looking up from the computer screen, he motioned for her to come around to his side of the desk. "There's something here I think you'll want to see."

When she rounded the desk, she glanced at the computer monitor. It wasn't even turned on. But before she could question why he'd been intently focused on a blank screen, he turned his chair sideways, wrapped his arms around her waist and pulled her down to sit on his lap.

"Good lord, Luke, what are you doing?" She'd assumed that his hands-off attitude at the office had been to keep from feeding the ever-present rumor mill. "What if someone notices your door is shut?"

"No one will think anything is out of the ordinary," he said, nipping at the sensitive skin along the column of her neck. When he leaned back to look at her, his grin was as promising and wicked as she'd ever seen it. "I'm the boss and you're my executive assistant. It's not at all unusual for us to have a private meeting with the door closed."

"That's true, but what about—"

When his mouth covered hers, Haley abandoned

trying to reason with him. Luke still hadn't informed anyone about their marriage beyond his twin brother. But she wasn't surprised when he told her on the way back to Nashville that he'd let Jake know about their arrangement. Being mirror twins, they had always shared a special bond.

As Luke began to nibble at the corner of her mouth, coaxing her to open her lips for him, she relegated all thought of his relationship with his brother to the back of her mind and responded to his unspoken request. As his tongue slipped inside to mate with her own, liquid fire raced through her veins and an exciting little charge of electric current began to gather into a need deep in the pit of her belly.

He moved his hands to lift her arms to his shoulders, giving him free access to her breasts and emitting a tiny moan, she arched into his palms. His taste, his tender teasing and the feel of his hands gently caressing her caused a delightful tightening in her lower stomach and she wished with all of her heart they were somewhere besides the Garnier office.

"Do you know what I think?" he prompted, when he finally broke the kiss.

He expected her to form a rational thought after a kiss like that and with his hands still holding her breasts, his thumbs still gently circling her nipples through her clothing?

Laying her head on his shoulder, she kissed his neck. His whole body shuddered and a tiny feminine thrill coursed through her at the knowledge that she could affect him that way.

"I don't have a clue what you have on your mind, but

I'm sure you're going to tell me," she whispered close to his ear.

"I'm thinking that I'd like to take you home for lunch," he stated, his tone hoarse.

"Really? And just what would be on the menu?" she inquired, leaning back to give him a wide-eyed innocent look.

The hunger in his incredibly blue eyes caused her stomach to do a funny little backflip. "You."

"I would love to go home for your kind of lunch," she agreed, regretting what she was about to say next. "But we have a luncheon meeting scheduled with Ray Barnfield to go over the figures for his new office building and I doubt he'd be very happy if we called to reschedule. And since we don't have a signed contract yet, he might even decide to go with another construction company."

"Damn, I forgot about that." Luke looked as disappointed as she felt. "No, rescheduling is completely out of the question. We've worked too hard on this project to risk losing it now."

"I assume you still want me to go along?" When the meeting had been set up, he'd mentioned as much.

He nodded. "I want you to present the materials estimates to Ray, then I'll jump in with the projected deadlines and close the deal."

Over the past five years, they'd worked out a system of presenting proposals to potential clients as a team and it had proven to be very effective, winning several lucrative contracts for Garnier Construction.

"I'll get Ray's file ready," she indicated as she started to get off Luke's lap.

"Hey, where do you think you're going?" he chided, tightening his hold on her.

"The meeting is scheduled for one o'clock." Smiling, she pressed a kiss to his lean cheek. "And if you expect me to help you bring this deal to a satisfactory end, I need to have all of my ducks in a row."

He gave her a quick kiss, then set her on her feet. "While you're getting everything lined out for the meeting, there's something else I want you to do."

"What would that be?"

His expression held a wealth of promise. "Call and cancel my appointments for the rest of the day and arrange for Ruth Ann to take over for you as well."

She had a pretty good idea why they were taking the afternoon off but felt compelled to ask, "Is there a reason we won't be back in the office this afternoon?"

"Once we leave the restaurant, we'll both be going home for dessert." His wide grin promised an afternoon of sheer ecstasy. "If you'll remember, we have a baby to make, sweetheart. And I'm taking immense pleasure in this little project."

Careful not to wake him, Haley slipped from beneath Luke's arm and got out of bed to search for her robe. Her tears were not only threatening, they were imminent and walking out onto the master suite's balcony, she let them flow freely down her cheeks as she considered what had taken place earlier in the day.

The meeting with the client couldn't have gone better. Together, she and Luke had presented plans and a cost estimate that enticed Mr. Barnfield and by the end of the luncheon, the man had verbally agreed to have

Garnier Construction build his new high-rise. Then, when she and Luke had left the restaurant, he'd brought her home and they'd spent the rest of the afternoon and most of the evening making slow, passionate love.

But for her, the day had been bittersweet. When they'd arrived at the restaurant, Luke hadn't introduced her to the client as Haley Garnier. He'd seemed to stress the point that she was Miss Rollins, his executive assistant.

She knew she was being completely unreasonable about the matter. But it still hurt to think that she was married to the man she loved with all of her heart and he couldn't find it within himself to tell anyone that she was his wife. Even if it was temporary.

How could he be so caring and considerate when they made love and not acknowledge her as his spouse?

Swiping at the tears running down her cheeks, she walked over to the railing to stare out at the night sky. She'd known when she agreed to have his baby that their marriage was an appeasement—a way to get her to go along with his plan.

But he hadn't even bothered to buy her a wedding ring. Would it be such a crime for him to refer to her as his wife for however long their union lasted? Couldn't he at least give her that much?

"What are you doing out here, Haley?"

At the sound of Luke's voice, she quickly tried to wipe away the evidence of her emotions with the back of her hand. "I just needed a little fresh air. I hope I didn't wake you."

"No. What woke me was rolling over and not finding you there beside me where you're supposed to be."

When he came up behind her and wrapped his arms

around her waist to pull her back against his chest, she closed her eyes and willed away a fresh wave of tears. No matter how he introduced her to people or how brief their marriage, she was in his arms now and she would have to content herself with that fact.

"What's wrong, sweetheart?" he asked, holding her close.

"N-nothing."

"Don't give me that. You've been crying. I can hear it in your voice." Turning her to face him, he shook his head. "And I want to know why."

Unable to meet his questioning look for fear of giving herself away, she focused on his wide bare chest. "Women cry for a variety of reasons. It doesn't necessarily mean that there's something wrong."

He tilted her chin up until their gazes met. "Could one of those reasons be a hormonal thing?"

"Sometimes."

Looking thoughtful, he stared at her for several long seconds. "Do you think we've achieved our goal?"

"It's probably too early for any symptoms indicating that I'm pregnant."

He was silent for several moments before his amiable expression turned to a dark frown, as he contemplated something.

"Luke?"

Taking a deep breath, he finally explained. "When Jake called the other night, it wasn't just to catch up with each other. He told me he'd talked to Arielle and she was sobbing her heart out. But she wouldn't tell him why." He shook his head. "We figured something had to be wrong."

"I suppose that could have been the case," Haley

conceded, nodding. "But women aren't like men. We don't keep things bottled inside. There are times when we cry simply to relieve tension and stress."

Luke mulled over what she'd said, then running his hands over her back in a soothing manner, he asked "Is that why you were crying just now?"

"Yes."

It was as good an excuse as any she could come up with. And in truth, she had been stressing. But his refusal to acknowledge her as his wife was something he wouldn't want to discuss.

"I think I know what you're worried about," he said, pulling her close.

"You do?" She seriously doubted he'd understand even if she told him what the problem was.

He nodded. "I'm sure it's normal to be frightened about getting pregnant and all the changes your body will go through." Kissing her tenderly, he held her to him. "But you aren't going to be alone, Haley. Unlike a lot of men, I don't consider my job finished once my son is conceived. I'll be with you throughout this whole thing."

The sudden tension she detected in his large frame confused her. "Is there something going on that I don't know about?" Haley asked.

Pausing, he finally took her by the hand, walked over to a grouping of patio furniture, then lowering himself into one of the wrought iron chairs, pulled her down to sit on his lap. "I believe I've told you before about me and Jake raising Arielle after our mother was killed in a car accident."

Haley nodded.

"Do you know why we were left with that responsibility, instead of our father taking care of our sister?" When she shook her head, he continued. "Because the bastard wasn't anywhere around. He took off shortly after our mother learned she was pregnant with Arielle. The same as when he learned she was expecting me and Jake."

"Your father left your mother—"

"Twice," he finished for her. "She loved him with all of her heart and trusted that he cared the same way about her. But all she got out of the bargain was three kids to raise alone and the heartache of watching the jerk continually walk out on her."

With sudden clarity, Haley saw the reason behind Luke's avoidance of relationships. He obviously never intended for anyone to have that kind of power over him.

"Oh, Luke, I'm so sorry. That must have been so difficult for all of you."

He shrugged his shoulders. "There's no reason to be sorry. We did just fine on our own and I'm thoroughly convinced we were better off without him."

She didn't know what to say. Her father might have completely ignored her after her mother had left Haley on his doorstep, but he'd at least furnished a roof over her head and food for her to eat. Apparently, Luke's father hadn't even bothered to stick around long enough to see to his children's basic needs.

"But the story doesn't end there," Luke continued, staring out at the gardens beyond the balcony railing. "We recently learned our mother wasn't the only woman to fall for his line of bull."

"You have another sibling?" she guessed.

Shaking his head, he sighed heavily. "More like

three. All brothers. All from different mothers. And all from different parts of the country."

Shocked, Haley could well understand his bitterness. "Your father certainly believed in sowing his share of wild oats, didn't he?"

"Oh, yeah." Luke was silent a moment before he went on. "I suppose you could consider Jake and I the lucky ones. At least we got to meet the man once when we were ten. The others never had that opportunity. They didn't even know his name."

"Why did your father return after all those years?" she interjected.

"He just showed up at the house one day, stuck around long enough to impregnate our mother with Arielle, then took off again." A chill slithered up her spine at the sound of Luke's harsh laughter. "Of course, Jake and I may have met him, but we didn't really know who he was, either. It wasn't until we learned about our half brothers that we discovered he'd been using an alias when he was with our mother. Instead of the starving artist he'd portrayed himself to be, he was a notorious womanizer with a bottomless bank account."

"When and how did you find out about your brothers if they didn't know who their father was?" she queried.

"After he was killed in a boating accident somewhere in the Mediterranean, our paternal grandmother hired a team of private investigators to look into her son's past escapades to see what damage he'd left in his wake throughout the years. She knew all along about the other three boys he'd fathered. But she only recently discovered that Arielle, Jake and I were also illegitimate grandchildren."

"That must have been heartbreaking for her," Haley

said, feeling compassion for the poor woman. "She was cheated out of watching all of you grow up and being part of your lives."

"Believe me, that old bird is a survivor," he corrected, his tone indicating he had no pity for his grandmother. "She probably wouldn't have taken the time to pay much attention to us anyway."

They fell silent for several minutes before Luke asked "Now that you've learned all about my family secrets, what about you? Why wasn't your mother part of the family picture?"

His question caused a knot to form in the pit of Haley's stomach. Millie Sanford may have given her life, but the woman had never been a mother to Haley.

"There really isn't a lot to tell," she began, wondering if Millie ever regretted her decision to give away her baby girl. "Shortly after I was born, she showed up and told my father that I was the product of their one-night stand and she was going to put me up for adoption if he didn't want to claim me."

"I'm sorry, sweetheart." Luke's arms tightened around her. "But if she didn't intend to keep you, why did she go through with the pregnancy?"

Haley had asked herself that a thousand times over the years and never came up with any answers. "I don't really know. I've often wondered if she thought she'd make it on her own with a baby, then decided it was too difficult once I was born. Or maybe she gave me up because she wanted me to have all the opportunities she couldn't give me."

His strong hands massaged the tension in her lower back. "I'm sure it was something like that."

She sighed. "But if that had been the case, you'd think she would have stayed in touch with my father to see how I was doing throughout the years."

"Have you tried to get in touch with her?" he asked, quietly.

"I've thought about it, but I don't even know where she went after she left me with Dad. Besides, what would I say? Oh, by the way, I'm the little girl you abandoned all those years ago." She shook her head. "If she'd wanted anything to do with me, I'm sure she'd have contacted me by now. After all, it's not like she didn't know who she left me with."

They fell silent before Luke asked "So it was just you and your dad all these years?"

"More like just me." She tried not to think of how lonely she'd felt growing up. "Dad was married to his work—always at the office or on a business trip—and even when he was at home, he never seemed to know what to do with me or how to relate to me. He left my care to our housekeeper, Mrs. Arnold."

"In other words, she raised you."

"Yes." Her chest tightened. "And now that I'm older, it's too late. My father passed away while I was in college and we'll never be able to have a relationship."

"Is that why it's so important for you to be a mother to the baby we're going to have?" Luke coaxed, his tone so gentle and caring that she couldn't stop a tear from slipping down her cheek.

"Yes." Suddenly feeling as if every ounce of her energy had been drained away, she laid her head on Luke's shoulder and snuggled into his embrace. "I don't ever want my child to go through the uncertainty of not feeling loved…and wanted," she revealed haltingly as sleep began to overtake her. "I intend for my baby to feel secure in the knowledge that she's the most…important person in my life."

Long after Luke heard Haley's breathing become shallow, indicating she'd drifted off to sleep, he sat holding her securely against him. He understood now more than ever why she'd been adamant about what it would take for her to have his son and why she'd insisted on joint custody. She wanted to protect his heir from the same type of loveless existence she'd been forced to grow up in.

Cradling her to him like a small child, he rose from the chair and carried her into his bedroom. He and his siblings had been lucky compared to Haley. They might not have had a father, but they'd had each other and they'd certainly known their mother. From the moment they were born until the day she died, Francesca Garnier had devoted herself to her children and left them with no doubt about how much they meant to her.

But Haley hadn't had that kind of childhood. She'd had no one to love her the way a child needed to be loved.

As he placed her on the bed, then stretched out beside her, Luke gathered her close. Emotions he wasn't at all comfortable with and certainly wasn't about to acknowledge filled his chest almost to the point of bursting.

But he stubbornly willed them away. He'd seen firsthand the emotional pain his mother suffered when his father rejected her love and there wasn't a chance in hell that he'd ever open himself up to that level of devastation.

Haley was a warm, compassionate woman who had

a lot of love to give and deserved a man with the capacity to love and cherish her just as much in return. Unfortunately, he just wasn't the right man for the job.

"Mr. Lucien Garnier, please hold for a call from Mrs. Emerald Larson."

Luke rolled his eyes at the sound of the stiff, formal voice of Emerald's personal assistant, Luther Freemont.

"Lucien, I'm so glad I caught you before you left the office for the day," Emerald said, coming on the line. "Did the transition from our management to yours go as smoothly as anticipated?"

"There were a couple of minor issues with the labor force, but nothing I couldn't straighten out," he responded, wondering why the old girl was fishing for answers from him, when they both knew she still had her share of loyal contacts in the Laurel offices.

"Excellent. I'm happy to hear things are moving along on that front."

"But you aren't calling to find out how I've done with Laurel Enterprises, are you?" Luke asked, running out of patience.

"No, I'm not."

"Why *are* you calling, Mrs. Larson?" he demanded.

"Considering our relationship, don't you think calling me 'Mrs. Larson' is bit formal, Lucien?"

"I've only known about you for a few weeks. Surely you don't expect me to call you Grandmother," he declared. "I told you when we first met that building a relationship at this stage of the game would be next to impossible."

"And I completely understand," she agreed, sounding

as if she really meant it. "If you'd like, why don't you call me Emerald, dear."

"All right, Emerald. And for the record, most people call me Luke."

"I prefer calling you by your given name."

"You'll do whatever pleases you anyway," he retorted, using his hand to rub the tension building at the base of his neck.

She laughed. "Of course, I will."

"Now that we have that settled, to what do I owe the pleasure of this call, *Emerald?*" he asked, wishing he'd ducked out of the office ten minutes earlier. If he had, he wouldn't be having this chitchat with her.

"I'm going to be in Nashville this weekend and I would very much like for you to attend a reception being held in my honor." She paused. "Your three other brothers will be in attendance and this would be an excellent opportunity for you, Jake and Arielle to meet them."

"Half brothers," Luke corrected.

"Yes, of course." To her credit, the old gal didn't even try to pretend she was offended by his bluntness and continued as if he hadn't pointed out the obvious. "Arielle is coming with me from San Francisco to fly into Nashville and I'm certain your twin brother plans to come from Los Angeles for the occasion. Will I be able to count on you, as well?"

He should have known when they all agreed to Emerald's offer that it would come with a considerable amount of strings. "I'll have to check my calendar and get back with you," he hedged.

"Wonderful. I'll expect to see you at eight on Saturday evening in the main ballroom at the Gaylord Opryland

Hotel." Before he pointed out that he hadn't committed to anything, she added, "And of course it goes without saying you're more than welcome to bring a guest."

"Of course," he repeated, rolling his eyes once more.

"I look forward to seeing you again, Lucien. Goodbye."

As he hung up the phone, he shook his head. He had to give her credit for one thing: Emerald Larson was damned good at getting what she wanted. Unless he missed his guess, Jake had been fed the same line of bull about her being certain Luke would be attending and now they'd both been roped in.

But the more he thought about it, the more it could work to their advantage. If Arielle was going to be there, maybe he and Jake could pull her aside and get to the bottom of what was going on with her.

And Luke had no doubt she was hiding something. She'd been avoiding his calls the past couple of weeks and that was the longest they'd ever gone without talking.

Checking his watch, Luke turned off his computer and rolled down his shirt sleeves. Haley had left an hour ago to run a couple of errands and it was time he called it a day, as well. He had a soft, sweet woman waiting on him at home. And he couldn't wait to get their evening started.

Eight

"It's negative," Haley announced, peering at the results window on the little white stick in her hand.

"Are you sure these things are accurate?" Luke asked, looking over her shoulder. "Maybe another brand would be better."

"From everything I've read, this test is the most accurate," she answered, checking the back of the box for the second time.

She picked up the instruction insert from the early pregnancy test and read through it again. "It says to retest a few days later if there are doubts about the results."

"You might still be pregnant." He grinned as they walked out of the master bathroom and over to the bed. "And in the meantime, all we have to do is relax and enjoy each other."

She smiled. "I'm sure you're up for the challenge."

Wrapping her in his arms, he rested his forehead against hers. "I can't help myself. You're just so damned desirable when you wake up. And when you walk into my office with my coffee. And—"

"I think I get the idea," she said dryly as she crossed the room to remove her robe and get into bed. "You're blaming me for your insatiable needs."

"I didn't have this problem before we started making love," he countered, walking over to remove his watch and place it in a small tray on top of the dresser. His grin turned positively wicked. "Do you know why I spend so much time sitting behind my desk at the office?"

Propping her pillow against the headboard, she leaned back against it. "I assume it's because you're working."

"Nope." He walked over to his side of the bed. "It's because I've been watching you or thinking about making love to you and I'm too aroused for people not to notice."

"So you're saying we can't go out in public together anymore?" she teased.

He shook his head as she watched him lower his boxers. "No, but when we are out, I find that I'd rather be here making love to you." He paused. "And speaking of going out in public together, I almost forgot to tell you about the reception on Saturday evening at the Opryland Hotel."

"For anyone I know?" she asked, shamelessly watching him. She loved his body, loved watching the play of muscles as he moved. It was just so darned sexy.

"You don't know her, but you do know *of* her," he commented, climbing into bed. "It's Emerald Larson."

Turning on his side to face her, he pulled her close. "But I don't want to talk about her now. I have more exciting things on my mind."

"Oh, really?" Haley couldn't keep from smiling at the promise on his handsome face and completely abandoned all thought as his firm lips nibbled and coaxed with a skill that stole her breath.

But when his tongue parted her lips to deepen the kiss, it felt as if he'd ignited a pyrotechnic display within her soul. A flickering light danced behind her closed eyes and a delicious warmth flowed through her veins as he stroked the inner recesses of her mouth, then encouraged her to explore him in kind.

Tasting and teasing him as he'd done her, her pulse quickened when she felt him reach for the lace hem of her gown. The feel of his palm as he slid it up her thigh and over her stomach to the underside of her breast, sent a searing current of heat dancing over every nerve in her body. But when he cupped her fully and lightly brushed his thumb over her hardened nipple, the heated desire swirling inside her quickly turned into a hungry flame.

She wanted him with a fierceness that she never imagined and running her hands over his side, then his hip, she took him in her palm to explore his length and the power of his need for her. She felt his entire body shudder a moment before he broke the kiss, then leaned back and shook his head.

"It's been brought to my immediate attention that one of us is overdressed for what we're about to do here," he said, sounding winded.

"Since you're the one not wearing anything, I suppose that would make me the guilty party."

Toying with the neck of her gown, his smile turned into a wicked grin a moment before he used both hands to rip the light cotton fabric all the way down to the hem.

"I'm not going to have any nightgowns left," she complained, not in the least bit upset.

His promising grin stole her breath. "Not that you're going to be needing them anytime soon, but if you insist, I'll buy you new ones." Quickly dispensing with her tattered nightgown, he hooked his thumbs under her panties. "And we definitely don't need these, either."

Raising her hips to help, a wave of electrifying desire covered every inch of her as he slid the offending garment down her legs, then tossed them over the side of the bed to the floor. Her wildest fantasies could not compare to the erotic thrill Luke created every time he removed her clothes.

"I don't know why you bother with them anyway. You know I'm just going to take them off of you," he said, pulling her against him.

"But you told me you enjoyed doing just that."

"Getting you out of your clothes is part of the fun." He frowned suddenly. "But I don't want to dwell on that now. Where were we before getting you out of your clothes became the big issue?"

"I believe you were going to explain why I don't need nightgowns and panties," she reminded, suddenly feeling quite breathless.

"No, I believe I told you that I intended to show you." He lightly brushed her lips with his as he pressed himself even closer.

Her eyelids drifted shut as she relished the feel of their bodies pressed close. His hard contours against her much softer curves excited her as little else could and sent a tremor of sheer delight straight through her to gather into a pool of need deep inside.

"Open your eyes, Haley."

When she did, the intense look in his eyes caused her heart to pound erratically. Hunger, urgent and undeniable, sparkled in the vivid blue depths and just knowing that she'd created such deep need in him as well sent threads of heated passion twining throughout her entire being.

He continued to hold her gaze with his as without a word he slowly slid his hand down to her knee, then back up along the inside of her thigh. Ripples of desire skipped over every nerve in her body and an extreme restlessness began to overtake her. She needed to be one with him, to have him buried so deeply inside her that she lost sight of where she ended and he began.

"Please…Luke," she said, amazed at the sultriness in her own voice.

"Only if you promise me something," he warned, lifting her leg over his.

"What?" At that moment, she would promise him almost anything if he would quench the fire threatening to send her into total meltdown.

"I don't want you to close your eyes." Taking her hand in his, he helped her guide him to her. "I want you to look at me while I'm inside you, Haley." Easing his hips forward, his jaw tightened and his eyes began to blaze with a feral light as he slowly began to enter her. "I want to see the moment when you realize there's no turning back, that I'm going to take you over the edge and put my baby inside of you to love and nurture."

"I promise I'll try," she whispered, placing her hand

on his chest. The steady rhythm of his heart matched the beating of her own and in that moment she'd never felt closer to him.

Her soul filled to overflowing with love as he completely joined their bodies, then slowly began to move within her. His gaze continued to hold hers as he built the bond between them to a fevered pitch and sensations, exquisite and sweet, flowed through her.

But all too soon the connection grew, changing, evolving into something that Haley never wanted to end. A sudden delicious tightness gripped her body, then quickly shattered to send her spinning out of control. Shivering from the force of her release, she heard herself whimper his name as every cell in her being melted with pleasure and she clung to him to keep from being lost.

Feeling the sweet languor of fulfillment wash over her, she watched Luke's eyes darken a moment before his body stiffened and he crushed her to him. He thrust himself into her one final time and as she felt the honeyed warmth of his life force flow into her, she knew that she could never love any other man the way she loved Luke. He owned her heart, her body and her soul.

On Saturday evening as he waited for the doorman to announce his and Haley's arrival to the guests at Emerald's reception, Luke glanced at her and wondered for at least the hundredth time in the past three weeks why it had taken him so long to see how beautiful she was. Her long blond curls cascaded over her bare shoulders like a golden waterfall and the strapless black evening gown she wore accentuated her slender feminine form to perfection.

"Mr. Luke Garnier and Miss Haley Rollins," the doorman finally announced to the crowded ballroom.

He thought he felt Haley's body go rigid a moment before she placed her hand in the crook of his arm and they walked toward the receiving line where Emerald and several others stood waiting to greet them. But glancing again at her, Luke decided he'd imagined it. She looked as serenely beautiful as she had the day she'd walked down the aisle of the little chapel in Pigeon Forge to trustingly place her hand in his and become his...wife.

His heart stalled. Why had that particular word come to mind? It was one that, over the course of the past several weeks, he'd been extremely careful to avoid.

"Lucien, darling, I'm so happy you decided to attend," Emerald greeted him, placing her bejeweled hand on his cheek and bringing him back to the present. Turning to Haley, she smiled. "And what a lovely young woman you're with this evening."

"This is my executive assistant, Haley Rollins," he introduced automatically. "Haley, I'd like you to meet Emerald Larson."

"How do you do, Ms. Rollins?" Emerald replied, lightly kissing Haley's cheek.

"L-lovely. It's a pleasure to meet you, Mrs. Larson." Was his mind playing tricks on him or had he heard a slight quaver in Haley's voice?

"I hope you don't mind, but I'm going to steal my grandson away from you for a few moments," Emerald declared, smiling. "There are a few people I would like for him to get acquainted with."

Luke could have cheerfully choked the old girl for dropping that little bomb. He'd avoided telling Haley that Emerald was the grandmother he'd mentioned. For one thing, theirs was a business arrangement and he hadn't felt it pertinent to their situation. And for another, he hadn't gotten used to the idea himself. Now, short of creating a scene, there was nothing he could do but allow Emerald to lead him away from Haley and over to the three men standing across the ballroom.

"Of course, I don't mind," Haley murmured, but her look clearly stated otherwise.

"I'll be right back," he whispered in her ear. "I promise that I'll explain all of this later."

She leaned away from him a fraction of an inch. The movement was ever so slight, but he'd noticed it just the same as if she'd fully recoiled from him. "Don't worry about me, I'll be fine. Take all the time you like," she professed, turning to walk in the opposite direction.

Unless he missed his guess, he was in hot water and other than omitting the fact that Emerald Larson was his grandmother, he couldn't figure out why.

"Your assistant is quite beautiful, Lucien," Emerald commented as they walked across the ballroom. "I take it there's more between the two of you?"

"That's really none of your concern, Emerald," he retorted, not at all surprised that she felt entitled to know about every aspect of his life. After all, she was the all-knowing, all-seeing Emerald Larson.

"Of course it is," she sweetly disagreed, smiling. "I'm your grandmother and I naturally want to see that you're happy." She placed her hand on his arm. "And if there's anything I can do to help, please don't hesitate to let me know."

"I seriously doubt that I'll need your assistance," he disclaimed, wondering what the hell she thought she could do that he couldn't.

"Just keep that in mind if you ever do," she reminded as they continued to cross the ballroom.

Her comments had him wondering how much she knew about his arrangement with Haley, but he didn't have time to dwell on it as they approached the three men.

"Lucien, I'd like for you to meet your brothers, Caleb Walker, Nicholas Daniels and Hunter O'Banyon," Emerald said. "Now, while you boys get to know each other, I'll return to my guests."

"She's a piece of work, isn't she?" Hunter asked, shaking his head as they watched Emerald walk back toward the ballroom entrance.

"Is she ever," Luke agreed, liking the man instantly.

"We're glad to get to know you and the rest of the Garnier side of the family," Caleb spoke up.

"Likewise," Luke answered, shaking hands with all three of his half brothers. "For the record, everyone but Emerald calls me Luke."

"Yeah, she insists on calling me 'Nicholas' most of the time," Nick disclosed, his expression reflecting his displeasure.

"When you have her kind of money, you can do anything you damned well please," Hunter summarized, laughing.

"I hear you own one of the biggest construction companies in the South and thanks to Emerald you've recently ventured into log homes," Nick described, sounding thoughtful. "Have you ever considered building in the western states? I promised my wife a new house for our anniversary and who better to build it than one of my brothers."

Luke smiled. "I haven't ventured past the Mississippi, but that doesn't mean I'm not open to the idea. If you're going to be in town for a few days, maybe we can get together."

"Save a spot at that table for me," Hunter added. "I run an air med-evac service in southwest Texas and I'd like to build an office and sleeping quarters for the on-duty crew separate from the hanger where we service the helicopters."

"And me," Caleb interjected. "You never know, I might just decide to have you build something for me out in New Mexico."

Luke had tried to tell himself that he didn't care if he ever met his half brothers. But truth to tell, he was glad for the opportunity. It wasn't their fault they had been thrown into the same set of circumstances that he, Jake and Arielle found themselves.

"How does Monday evening sound?" he asked. All three men agreed, and naming a time and place, Luke added, "I'll see if Jake will be able to rearrange his schedule and hang around another day or two and join us."

"Sounds good," Hunter confirmed, glancing toward a group of women. "Uh-oh, I think Callie's trying to get my attention again."

"Yeah, Alyssa's giving me one of those looks, too," Caleb noted, smiling toward a pretty auburn-haired woman across the ballroom.

"Then I'll see you Monday evening," Luke said.

When he turned to find Haley, Luke spotted her by the buffet table. Damned if that jerk Chet Parker wasn't standing right beside her. What the hell was *he* doing at a reception for Emerald? And did the guy have some kind of radar honed in on Haley wherever they went?

"Looks to me like the entertainment for this little bash is about to make time with your new wife," Jake taunted, coming up to stand beside Luke.

Glancing at his brother, he felt as if he was looking in a mirror. But instead of wearing a devil-may-care grin like Jake, Luke was certain his expression bordered on premeditated murder.

"He's the entertainment for the evening?"

"That's what I hear." Rocking back on his heels, Jake nodded and took a sip of the drink he held. "You do know he's most likely looking for wife number four?"

"I've heard the rumor," Luke responded, his gaze never wavering from the pair at the buffet table.

"I represented his second wife in their divorce and let me tell you, she came away with a bundle," Jake supplied, sounding quite pleased with himself.

"Good for you," Luke commented absently. He felt his blood pressure skyrocket when he watched Parker put his hand on Haley's bare shoulder. "I'll be back in a few, Jake. Right now, I have something I need to take care of."

His brother chuckled. "Let me know if you need back up with that, bro."

When he walked up and slipped his arm around Haley's waist, Luke made it a point to meet Parker's questioning gaze head on. "Haley, have you seen my sister?"

"I spoke to her a few minutes ago," she answered, her tone as cool as he'd ever heard it.

"Why don't you go find her for me?" he proposed, his gaze never wavering from Parker's. "I'd like to talk with her before we leave."

Haley glared at him for several seconds, before giving him a short nod. "Of course, Mr. Garnier. Whatever you say, Mr. Garnier."

She was less than happy when she brushed past him, but he'd straighten out things with her later. At the moment, he had to put the fear of God into one country Casanova.

"Listen up, Parker. I'm only going to tell you this once," Luke threatened, his jaw clenched so tight it felt welded shut. "Stay the hell away from Haley."

"Why should I?" Parker demanded, his tone self-assured. "You seem to keep forgetting that you bring her to these things or else she wouldn't be wandering about alone." He smiled. "A little gal like Haley makes a man think about settling down and raising a couple of kids."

"I know, that's why I married her."

"She's your wife?" Parker shook his head. "She's not wearing a ring. If you're married, why isn't she wearing your brand?"

Making a mental note to remedy that problem as soon as possible, Luke glared at the man. "That's my business, not yours. She's mine and you keep your damned hands off her."

"And if I don't?" Parker prompted, his cocky grin sending Luke's blood pressure into stroke range.

"You'll be picking up several of those capped teeth

of yours from the floor," Luke warned, halfway hoping the man would give him a reason to show that he meant business.

"Is that a threat?" Parker asked, raising an eyebrow.

Luke shook his head. "No, it's a fact."

Luke walked away before he carried out his promise and punched Parker square in the face. Taking several deep breaths to bring his anger under control, he searched the crowd for Haley. He wasn't sure who he was irritated with the most—Parker for zooming in on the fact that Haley wasn't wearing a wedding band or himself for forgetting to buy her one.

Either way, it didn't change the fact that she belonged to him, and Luke Garnier wasn't the type of man who shared what was rightfully his.

By the time Haley found Arielle in the powder room, her anger at Luke had been replaced with an undeniable sadness. There was no way he'd ever see their marriage as anything more than another one of his business deals. She'd been deluding herself when she'd thought that he might.

Not only had he introduced her to Emerald Larson as his executive assistant, he obviously hadn't shared the fact that the woman was his newfound grandmother. And if that wasn't proof enough that he viewed her only as his employee, just look at the way he'd ordered her to look for his sister.

"Haley, are you all right?" Arielle asked, clearly concerned. "You don't look like you feel very well. Should I go get Luke?"

Lowering onto one of the plush sofas in the lounge

area, Haley shook her head. "I'm fine, really. And no, I'd rather not see Luke at the moment."

"Uh-oh." Arielle walked over to sit down beside her. "What has that boneheaded brother of mine done now?"

"More like what he hasn't done," Haley informed, feeling absolutely miserable.

She wanted a baby more than anything, but what had she gotten herself into? How could marrying a man she loved with all of her heart for the purpose of having the baby she wanted so badly, make her feel so hopeless?

"You love him, don't you?" Arielle inquired, reaching to place her hand on Haley's. "That's why you agreed to his hair-brained plan to have a baby, isn't it?"

"You know about our arrangement?" she ventured, somewhat surprised.

"I know all about it," Arielle assured Haley, her smile encouraging. "When Luke told Jake about the two of you getting married and the plan to have a baby, Jake couldn't dial my number fast enough." She grinned. "I think it was just too much for poor Jake to keep to himself. But it did give me a bit of a reprieve."

"I'm sure it was quite a shock to both of you," Haley attested, nodding. "But enough about me and Luke. What about you? Your brothers—"

Obviously not wanting to discuss her brothers' concerns, Arielle interrupted, "I've known for some time that you absolutely adore Luke."

"But how? I've always been careful not to show how I felt about him."

The young woman smiled. "When I was here at Christmas, I saw the way your eyes would light up when he walked into the office. And let's face it, women are a lot more intuitive than men. You could hang a sign around your neck, advertising how much you care about him and I think Luke would probably miss it."

"Men are rather clueless, aren't they?" Haley agreed, her mood lightening ever so slightly.

Arielle nodded. "And Luke is one of the worst. When it comes to business, he's unsurpassed. But he's avoided having a real relationship so long that he doesn't recognize what is as plain as the nose on his face to the rest of us. I'm just glad he finally realized how perfect you are for him."

"You do know that our marriage is just to get me to have his heir? It's only temporary," Haley elaborated, wondering if Luke's sister really did know everything.

"That's what I was told, but I don't think that's going to be the case." Arielle gave Haley a knowing look. "I saw the way Luke reacted when he found Chet Parker talking to you. If looks could kill, they would be hauling poor old Chet to the morgue right now."

"But I've never been interested in anyone but Luke," Haley argued, shaking her head.

Arielle laughed. "I know that and you know that, but my overly obtuse brother can't see it."

They were silent for a few moments, before Haley brought up her brothers' concern. "I'm sure you know Luke and Jake are very worried about you."

The young woman sighed as she stared down at her hands. "As much as I love my brothers and appreciate everything they've done for me, there are some things they just can't fix."

Haley put her arm around Arielle shoulders. "Is there anything I can do?"

Shaking her head, Arielle raised tear-filled eyes to meet Haley's questioning gaze. "I really don't think there's anything anyone can do. I'm almost three months pregnant."

"Have you told the baby's father?" Haley asked, her heart going out to her sister-in-law.

"I've tried, but I can't find him." Arielle bit her trembling lower lip. "Please, you have to promise me you won't tell Luke or Jake. I'm just not ready to listen to a lecture right now."

"You have my word." She wasn't about to betray her sister-in-law's confidence. "But you will have to tell your brothers eventually."

"I know, but I have some things that I need to work out before I let them know." Sniffing, Arielle straightened her shoulders. "Besides, Luke and Jake would just start demanding to know who the father is so they could have one of those famous brotherly talks with him."

"You're right. And that would probably just make matters worse." Haley knew for certain they'd track the man down no matter what it took.

"My brothers don't seem to realize that I'm not ten years old anymore and these are my decisions to make, not theirs."

"If you need to talk to anyone, you know I'm as close as the nearest phone," Haley attested. She truly liked Arielle and hoped they would remain friends even after she and Luke parted ways.

"Thank you, Haley," Arielle reflected, hugging her. "I hope Luke wakes up soon and realizes how much he loves you. I really would like to keep you for my sister."

Haley tightly closed her eyes to keep a fresh wave

of tears in check as she hugged Arielle, too. She greatly appreciated her sister-in-law's good wishes, but she really held no hope for that ever happening.

Nine

On Monday evening, Luke guided Haley to the private room he'd reserved at the restaurant for the dinner meeting with his brothers, and holding the chair for her, smiled at his brothers and their wives. "Sorry we're late, but there was an accident on I-24 and we had to make a detour."

"Don't worry about it," Caleb spoke up. "We all just got here ourselves."

"Why don't you introduce your lovely date?" Jake teased, his knowing grin enough to set Luke's teeth on edge. "I've known Haley for several years, but I don't think you had the chance to introduce her to anyone at Emerald's reception."

"This is my executive assistant, Haley Rollins," Luke announced, seating himself beside her. "Haley, these are my brothers, Caleb, Nick and Hunter and their wives Alyssa, Cheyenne and Callie."

With the introductions complete, he noticed that Haley had grown extremely quiet. "Are you feeling all right?" he whispered, leaning close to her ear.

"I'm fine," she murmured, then immediately turned away to engage the other women at the table in conversation.

Deciding that getting to the bottom of what was wrong with her would have to wait until after they returned home, Luke spent an enjoyable evening getting better acquainted with his brothers. They hadn't known each other for more than a couple of days, but he knew they were building a lifelong bond and looked forward to staying in touch with them. He was also pleased to see that over the course of the evening, Haley's mood had improved. She seemed to have opened up and was enjoying the company of his sisters-in-law, as well.

"So, when are we all getting together again?" Hunter asked as the men's conversation about their various building projects began to wind down.

"If you'd like to come out to Wyoming this summer for a week or two, Cheyenne and I would love to have the company," Nick offered. "We'll give the old house a family send-off, then next summer we'll have a get-together and christen the new log home Luke's company is going to build for us."

"Absolutely," Cheyenne agreed enthusiastically. "And we'd love for you to come for a visit too, Haley."

"We all went up there last summer and had a great time," Alyssa Walker added, laughing. "I even learned to ride a horse."

"I'm sure you'd enjoy yourself, Haley," Callie O'Banyon proclaimed, smiling. "Please say you'll try."

Luke watched Haley give the women a weak smile. "That would be very nice, but I'm not sure what I'll be doing this summer. If it's all right, I'll have to let you know later."

No one besides himself and Jake seemed to think Haley's vague answer was anything out of the ordinary. But when they rose to leave, Jake made it a point to pull Luke aside.

"What's going on, bro? Why wouldn't Haley be right there with you?"

Luke shook his head. "I have a pretty good idea and you can bet your life I'm going to find out for certain."

As soon as they were comfortably seated in the back of his limo, Luke pushed the button to raise the privacy window between them and the driver. "You seemed to have a good time this evening."

She nodded. "I really like your brothers and their wives. They're all very nice."

Silence reigned for several more minutes before he asked what he thought might be the likely cause for her moodiness. "Are you still worried that we might not have been successful yet? Because if you are, don't be. I'm sure if you aren't pregnant this month, you will be shortly."

Instead of answering, she simply shrugged.

Trying to get her to open up to him was like trying to pull teeth and he was damned tired of it. "What's wrong? And don't tell me 'nothing' because you haven't been yourself for the past few days."

"I don't know what you mean." She wouldn't look him in the eye.

He shook his head. "Don't play dumb, sweetheart. We both know you're a lot more intelligent than that."

When she finally raised her gaze to meet his, the sadness in the turquoise depths caused his gut to twist into a tight knot. "If you don't mind, I'd rather not...go into it right now," she said.

He'd bet every last penny he had that she was a heart-beat away from the flood gates opening. "Okay, we'll wait until we get home," he concurred, putting his arm around her shoulders and drawing her close to his side. "But I want answers, Haley. And neither of us are going to get any sleep until I get them."

The rest of the ride home was spent in complete silence and when the driver finally opened the limousine's rear door and Luke helped her from the backseat, Haley's nerves were stretched to the breaking point. For the past several days, she'd been struggling with herself and having dinner with his brothers and their wives this evening had helped her reach a decision. What she had to say wasn't going to be easy and Luke certainly wasn't going to like hearing it, but she had no choice in the matter. Her survival depended on it.

While Luke locked the front door and set the security alarm, she slowly climbed the circular stairs to the second floor and steeled herself for the argument she knew was sure to ensue. She just hoped with all of her heart she could voice what had to be said before she dissolved into a torrent of tears or worse yet, allow him to convince her to change her mind.

When she entered the master suite, Luke wasn't far

behind and after he'd closed the French doors, she turned to look at the man she loved more than life itself.

"What's going on, Haley?" he asked before she had a chance to speak. "And don't try to deflect the question again, because we both know that something's bothering you."

Tossing her purse onto the bed, she took a deep fortifying breath. "I never thought I would go back on a promise to you, Luke. And God knows that having to say this to you now is killing me. But I just can't do this anymore. I thought I could, but I can't."

His eyes narrowed as he tugged his tie loose and released the button at the collar of his shirt. "And just what exactly is it that you think you can't do, Haley?"

"Th-this." She struggled to keep her voice even, but she knew she was failing miserably. "I can't continue this charade any longer."

"I think this would be a good time for me to remind you that we have a couple of written contracts," he countered, his tone so calm and collected she wanted to scream.

"You mean the prenuptial papers you had me sign?"

He nodded. "Those protect my assets and custody issues if we have a child."

"Don't worry about that," she disclosed, feeling more desolate and alone than she'd ever felt in her life. "I don't want anything from you. I just want out."

"We also have a marriage certificate. I was under the impression that made things very real. And let's not forget our verbal agreement for you to have my heir," he reminded. "In most courts, that's just as legal and binding as a written document, sweetheart."

Why did it not surprise her that he'd bring up the

threat of litigation if she tried to get out of it? But then, that's all their marriage had been to him, all it would ever be—a business deal to get what he wanted.

"Why are you doing this to me, Luke?"

"I'm not doing anything. You're the one who brought all of this up." He shrugged out of his suit coat and tossed it on a chair along with his tie. "You agreed to have my heir if I met your requirements." He started walking toward her. "I followed through with my end of the bargain and we got married. Now I fully expect you to follow through with yours and have my baby."

She held up her hand to stop his advance at the same time that she backed a few steps away. If he touched her, she knew for certain her resolve would crumble.

"Please don't, Luke. We both know this isn't a marriage. It's a…" She searched for a word to describe the biggest mistake she'd ever made. "…a farce, a sham, an outright degradation to the sanctity of marriage."

Folding his arms across his chest, he gave her a look she'd seen many times before. He was going into serious negotiation mode again. But this wasn't up for compromise.

"What do you think our marriage should be, Haley?" he asked calmly.

"Not this," she retorted, becoming more upset with each passing second. She walked over to the sitting area by the balcony doors to put more distance between them. "Whether it's a temporary situation or not, I'm your wife. But there hasn't been one single time that you've introduced me as anything more than your employee. Not to your clients. Not to your family. When you introduced me to your brothers and their wives this evening, you told them I was your executive assistant."

"And your point is?"

"We're supposed to be married. We live together. Sleep together. That makes me your—"

"So you're saying that you want me to start referring to you as my wife?" he interrupted.

How could he be so intelligent and still be so stubbornly insensitive?

"No. I want you to want to *think* of me as your wife."

"What makes you so sure I don't?"

Haley felt her stomach twist into a tight knot. He wasn't the type of man who conceded even the slightest point of an issue.

"Don't patronize me, Luke. If you thought of me as your wife, you'd introduce me to people that way. Instead of telling everyone my name is Haley Rollins, you'd tell them I'm Haley Garnier." She shook her head. "You couldn't possibly think of me as your wife. I don't even wear the basic symbol of marriage."

"A wedding ring?" he asked, his intense stare seeming to bore all the way to her soul.

"Y-yes," she said as a wave of dizziness washed over her.

"You told me the day we got married that it didn't matter that I hadn't bought you a ring," he argued, taking a step toward her.

As she fought the swirling sensation making her head pound, perspiration broke out on her forehead and she had a hard time focusing on what he'd said. "I tried to tell myself…that I didn't care…but God help me… I do."

"Why, Haley?" He took another step forward. "Why do you care so much? Why do you want me to tell people you're my wife? And why do you want to take my last name?"

The thundering roar in her ears made his voice sound as if it came from a very long distance. "B-because...I—"

"Haley!"

She heard him shout her name, but she couldn't speak and her limbs suddenly felt leaden. Swaying, she tried to focus on Luke rushing toward her, his arms outstretched.

But as the relentless spinning in her head pulled her further into the deep vortex, suddenly and without warning an excruciating pain shot through her temple and a split second later, everything went dark.

As he raced his Escalade through the dark streets of Nashville, Luke's heart pounded against his ribs with the force of a sledgehammer and his gaze never wavered from the back of the ambulance with its siren screaming and lights flashing just ahead of him. When he'd watched Haley turn ghostly pale and crumpled like a marionette with severed strings, he'd tried his damnedest to get to her, tried to keep her from going down. But she'd backed too far away from him and he hadn't had a chance of catching her before she fell and struck her head on the corner of the coffee table in the sitting area.

He took a deep shuddering breath. He would never, as long as he lived, forget the nightmarish sight of her limp, unconscious body on his bedroom floor, blood trickling down her pale cheek from the cut at her temple. And she hadn't yet regained consciousness.

When the ambulance finally turned into the emergency entrance of the hospital, Luke brought the SUV to a sliding halt not far behind and threw open the driver's door. He briefly noticed that he'd parked in a restricted zone, but he didn't give it a second thought as he ran toward the gurney being unloaded from the red and white vehicle. Let the police tow his car. He didn't care. All that mattered was getting to Haley and making sure that she received the best medical care that was humanly possible.

"Has she woken up?" he asked when the paramedics lifted the stretcher from the back of the ambulance and then rolled it through the automatic double doors into the hospital's emergency room.

"Not yet," one of the two men responded as they rushed past the nurse's station and wheeled the stretcher into a treatment room. The man's voice sounded grimmer than Luke cared to hear and fear twisted his gut into a tight knot.

"Sir, if you'll please come with me, I need to get some information from you," a woman instructed from somewhere behind him.

Turning to the nurse walking toward him, he shook his head. "Can't it wait until later? I don't want to leave her."

"I'm afraid not, sir." The woman gave him a sympathetic smile. "I know how worried you must be, but I need to get the patient's medical background from you. Now, if you'll please follow me, we can get this taken care in just a few minutes."

Luke looked at Haley through the window of the treatment room where a bevy of medical personnel had surrounded the narrow bed. There was a flurry of activity as tubes were unrolled, IVs were hung on metal poles and an oxygen mask was placed over her nose and mouth.

He shook his head again resolutely. "She needs me and I'm not leaving her."

"But sir, I have to get—"

Luke turned to glare at the woman. "Let's get this straight. You can ask me whatever you need to know right here and I'll do my best to give you the answers you need. But I'm not leaving her side. Understand?"

Realizing that she wasn't going to win, the nurse disappeared for a moment, then returned with several papers on a clipboard. Luke answered what little he knew about Haley's medical history, but when the woman wanted to know who to list as the next of kin, he had no problem giving her his name.

"And what is your relationship to the patient?" the woman asked.

Luke kept his gaze trained on the activity taking place in the treatment room. "I'm her husband."

Nodding, the nurse added it to the chart and started through the treatment room door to give the medical team the information. "The doctor will be out to talk with you as soon as he knows something, Mr. Garnier."

Luke continued to watch through the window as he thought about what he'd said to the nurse. In any other set of circumstances, he might have been surprised at how quickly the pronouncement had rolled off his tongue. But telling the nurse that he was Haley's husband had come as naturally as taking his next breath.

And that's when it hit him. He'd tried not to think

about it, denied it was happening and fought hard not to do it, but he'd fallen in love with her.

But before his realization could sink in, his heart stalled at the sight of a man in hospital scrubs walking out of the treatment room and heading straight for him.

"Mr. Garnier?"

"Is my wife going to be all right?" he demanded, tightness in his throat.

"I wish I could say she is, but at this point, we just aren't sure. We're going to have to do some tests before I can give you a prognosis." He reached out to shake Luke's hand. "My name is Dr. Milford and I'm the resident neurologist on call this evening. I'll be in charge of your wife's care and I'll do everything I can for her. But before we take her to Imaging, I need to know, is she pregnant or is there the possibility that she might be pregnant?"

"I'm not sure," Luke advised, feeling as if he was an unwilling participant in a horrific nightmare. "We've been trying to get pregnant, but I don't know if we've been successful."

The doctor nodded. "In that case, we won't risk doing a CT scan of the head because of radiation and the possible harm it could do to the fetus."

"I want you to do whatever you have to do to bring Haley out of this. Even if there is a baby and it comes down to a choice of tests to find out what's wrong, you do what's best for my wife," Luke directed without hesitation.

"We'll do an MRI and that will be safe for both of them, in case she is pregnant," Milford concluded, his voice filled with understanding.

As Luke watched, two nurses maneuvered Haley's bed through the door and out into the hall. "Where will you take her after the test?" he asked, wanting to be as close to her as possible.

"I'm having them ready a bed on the third floor. That's where we take care of our head trauma patients," Dr. Milford answered as he turned to follow the gurney. "She'll be taken there straight from Imaging and I'll meet you in the waiting room with the test results."

Getting directions from the nurse's station, Luke prayed like never before on the elevator ride to the third floor. When he found the waiting area closest to the room Haley would be taken to, he lowered himself into one of the chairs and ran a shaky hand over his face in an effort to keep his choking emotions in check. God, he couldn't lose her now, not when there was so much he needed to say to her, so much that he needed to make right between them.

What had made him so damned relentless with his questions? Why had it been so important that he force her to tell him what he'd known for weeks?

Haley was in love with him and had been for years. Hell, after getting to know her intimately this past month, he knew for a certainty that she would have never married him if she hadn't loved him.

And the ultimate irony of all of it was that he'd probably loved her just as long. He'd just been too blind to see it.

But even after he'd figured it out, he'd been an arrogant jerk about it. He'd known the hell he was putting her through, but he'd wanted her to be the one to admit her feelings, had been determined to get her to say the words first.

He reached into his pants pocket and withdrew the small black velvet box. Flipping it open, he stared at the white gold wedding band, with an array of sparkling white diamonds, that was nestled inside. He'd bought the ring just that morning and intended to surprise Haley with it right after they returned home from dinner with his brothers.

Why hadn't he bought it for her earlier? Why had he waited until Chet Parker goaded him into even thinking of it?

Luke snapped the box shut and stuffed it back into his pants pocket. He knew exactly why he'd finally purchased the ring. He'd wanted to send a message to dirtbags like Parker to keep their hands off of Haley.

He took a deep steadying breath. But now the ring meant so much more. Now the wedding band symbolized his love for Haley and his steadfast determination to make their arrangement—their marriage—permanent.

He just prayed to God that he had the chance to give it to her.

Ten

An hour after seeing the medical staff roll Haley's bed out of the treatment room for her MRI, Luke sat in the waiting room wondering what the hell was going on. The test seemed to be taking forever and the longer it took, the more worried he became.

"Mr. Garnier, if you'll follow me, we'll step into the consultation room to discuss your wife's test results and her prognosis," Dr. Milford said, motioning for Luke to follow him.

Lost in his own misery, Luke hadn't even noticed the man's approach. Jumping to his feet, he followed the man into the room and when the doctor closed the door behind them, sank into one of the chairs lining the consultation room wall.

"Is Haley going to be all right?" Luke asked without waiting for the doctor to speak.

"The MRI showed that your wife has a concussion, which we knew," Dr. Milford reported, sitting in a chair across from Luke. "And I'm relieved by the fact that we found no signs of bleeding in the brain and only a slight swelling."

"Has she regained consciousness?" Luke inquired, praying that she had.

Dr. Milford nodded. "She came to as we were taking her for the MRI."

"Thank God." Weak with relief, Luke drew some much needed air into his lungs. "How is she feeling now?"

"She's complaining of a headache, but that's common with a concussion and nothing to be overly alarmed about." He glanced at the chart in his hand. "We did have to close the wound at her temple with a couple of sutures and I want to keep her overnight for observation, but I see no reason she can't go home tomorrow—as long as she takes it easy for a few days, gets plenty of rest and has someone with her to watch for signs of complications."

"When can I see her?" Luke requested, rising to his feet. He needed to see for himself that Haley was really going to be all right.

"There's something else, Mr. Garnier," Dr. Milford added, his expression unreadable.

Unsure of what the doctor was going to say, Luke sank back down in the chair. "Is it something serious?"

Dr. Milford shook his head. "It's routine when someone is brought to the hospital to do a complete blood workup on the patient. Your wife's blood tests show that she is indeed pregnant, which could very well account for the fainting that caused her fall."

"Is that unusual?" Luke interjected, trying to

remember what he'd read on the Internet about the first few weeks of a woman's pregnancy.

"It's not uncommon for some women in their first trimester to have bouts of light-headedness," the doctor reassured, finally smiling.

Luke should have been ecstatic at the news that he and Haley had been successful, but at the moment, he was too relieved to give it a lot of thought. Just knowing that she was going to recover was all he could ask for.

"Anything else?" he asked.

Dr. Milford shook his head as he rose to leave. "Everything else checks out fine. She's in excellent health and I don't anticipate any further problems."

Thanking him, Luke shook the doctor's hand, then hurried down the hall toward Haley's room. There was so much he needed to say to her, so many things he wanted to explain. But it would have to wait until after he took her home. Besides the fact that she needed her rest, he needed time to make a few plans that he hoped would convince her of his sincerity when he told her how much he loved her and asked that she give him—and their marriage—a second chance.

As Haley waited for Luke to open the front door, then stepped back for her to enter the foyer of his mansion, hopelessness filled her all the way to her soul. He hadn't said more than a handful of words to her since arriving at the hospital to bring her home and the unfamiliar tension between them was about to kill her.

One of the nurses had told her that Luke spent the entire night in the chair beside her bed and commented about how devoted he was and how much he loved her.

But he hadn't been there when she'd wakened that morning and he'd only arrived at the hospital a few minutes before the final release papers were signed. And if that wasn't enough evidence that the problems between them were insurmountable, the fact that he hadn't once mentioned her pregnancy was.

"Do you feel like being up and about or do you need to lie down for a while?" he asked solicitously.

"No, I'd rather stay up for a while, if you don't mind."

"Whatever you feel like doing is fine." He led the way into the den, then standing there looking at her as if he was unsure of what to say next, he inquired, "How's your headache?"

"It's almost gone."

"That's good." Falling silent, he looked like he'd prefer to be anywhere else but in her presence.

"Luke, we have to stop this," she began, unable to bear another second of the strained tension between them.

Their overly polite conversation was driving her nuts. They were two strangers exchanging pleasantries, not a man and woman who had lived and loved together for the past month. And who now needed to discuss the fact that their marriage was at an end.

"I couldn't agree more. It's time we got everything out in the open and things settled between us." He pointed toward the chairs in front of the fireplace. "You're supposed to be taking it easy."

Lowering into one of the plush armchairs, she waited for him to sit down. When he remained standing, she gazed up at the man she still loved with all of her heart. She'd told herself that loving him the way she did would be enough for her, that it didn't matter if he couldn't care as deeply for her as she did him. But she had only been fooling herself. She wanted—needed—his love in return.

Unfortunately, Luke wasn't willing to open himself up to that type of relationship. And she'd come to the realization that she couldn't settle for less.

She took a deep breath. "We both know that there were a lot of things left unsaid last night."

He nodded as he leaned his shoulder against the fireplace and crossed his arms over his wide chest. "Where do you think we should start?"

"I should probably begin by telling you that I'm sorry, Luke. None of this is your fault. I accept full responsibility for making such a mess of things." She stared at her hands clenched into a tight knot in her lap. "You were right last night when you said you'd held up your end of the bargain. You've done everything I asked."

"So have you," he indicated, his voice strangely emotionless. "You're going to have my baby."

Thinking of the life she carried, Haley smiled and placed her hand over her flat stomach. "And I couldn't be happier about that. I've dreamed of the day when I would have a child of my own." Of having your child, she added silently.

"But?"

"I can't honor our agreement to stay married until after the baby is born," she disclosed, wondering how her heart could keep on beating even as it was breaking in two.

"But if I remember correctly, that was your main requirement for having my heir," he remarked, walking over to stand directly in front of her.

"And I'm sorry I got us both into this fiasco," she confessed, tears filling her eyes. "But if I don't get out of this now, I don't think I'd be able to survive our breaking up later on."

His expression turned thoughtful. "Is that the only reason you want me to give you a divorce?"

"Luke, please don't make this any more difficult than it has to be," she urged as she wiped an errant tear from her cheek.

He didn't want to hear the real reason she couldn't continue being his wife, wouldn't want to know that she was hopelessly in love with him and had been from the moment they met.

"Okay, you've had your say. Now, I intend to have mine," he declared, his voice as determined as she'd ever heard it. "You want a divorce because you're in love with me, admit it."

She wasn't surprised that he'd figured out how she felt about him. He'd had more than ample opportunity to come to that realization over the course of the past month. But did he have to humiliate her by pointing out that he didn't want her feeling the way she did about him?

"Yes, I love you," she admitted, finding it difficult to get her voice above a whisper. "I've loved you for years."

"Then before I give you my answer, there's something I think you need to know, Haley." Turning, he walked back to the fireplace and seemed to take an inordinate amount of interest in something on the mantel.

"I could have found someone else with similar characteristics, whom I could have convinced to have my heir," he explained, his back still to her. "But do you have any idea why it was so important to me that you be the mother of my baby?"

"No."

There was something in his tone that caused her heart to beat double time and a small bubble of hope to form within her soul. But she refused to allow it to grow. She wouldn't be able to bear the devastation if it turned out she was wrong.

He picked up whatever had claimed his attention on the mantel, then turning, walked over to kneel down in front of her. "The reason I didn't want any other woman having my baby, the reason I went along with your marriage stipulation and the reason I won't give you a divorce without a damned good fight is because I love you, too, Haley Garnier. More than life itself. It took me a long enough time to realize it, but I do and you might as well come to terms with the fact because I'm not letting you go that easily."

The hope she'd tried so hard to keep tamped down, blossomed and grew to fill her with a joy she'd never imagined possible. "Oh, Luke, I love you so much I ache with it," she revealed, reaching for him.

When he wrapped her in his arms to pull her close, she felt his body shudder and she knew he was experiencing the same emotion she was. "God, sweetheart, it like to have killed me when I thought there was a possibility that I might lose you."

"I'm so sorry I put you through that," she stated, kissing his cheek. "I thought the reason I started feeling ill was because I was so emotional. I had no idea about the baby."

He shook his head. "No, you have nothing to be sorry about. You were upset with me and rightly so. I've been a complete bastard not to consider your feelings in all of this."

"But you had no way of knowing how I felt," she said, loving him more with each passing second.

"Yes, I did." He cupped her cheeks with both hands and the love shining in his vivid blue eyes stole her breath and caused her heart to soar. "Maybe not consciously, but deep down I think I've always known. You wouldn't have even considered my proposition if you hadn't loved me."

Luke took her hand in his and the feel of his warmth and the strength of his love flowed through every part of her. "There's something I need to ask you, sweetheart."

"And what would that be, dear husband?" She loved finally having the freedom to call him that and to openly tell him how much she loved him.

His expression turned serious and so tender, it brought a fresh wave of tears to her eyes. "Will you marry me, Haley Rollins Garnier?"

"But, darling, we're already married."

"Marry me again," he stressed, showing her the object he'd removed from the mantel. He flipped open the top of the little black velvet box and removed a gorgeous diamond-encrusted, white gold wedding band. Then, holding it close to the third finger on her left hand, he asked "Will you do me the honor of becoming my wife again?"

"Yes, Luke. Nothing would make me happier." Her

heart filled to overflowing with love when he slid the ring onto her finger. As she gazed down at the sparkling diamonds, she couldn't believe that it was a perfect fit. "How did you know the size?"

He gave her a smile that caused her pulse to race. "I have my ways."

Kissing him until they both gasped for breath, she couldn't stop smiling. "Yes, Luke Garnier, I'll continue to be your wife for the rest of my life."

To her dismay, he shook his head. "Sweetheart, that's not what I asked you. I want to know if you'll marry me again."

She couldn't believe what she was hearing. "You mean you actually want us to go through another ceremony?"

He nodded as he pulled two folded pieces of paper from his pants pocket. Handing her one of them, he smiled. "This is the name and phone number of the wedding coordinator at the Opryland Hotel. As soon as you're feeling well enough, I want you to set up an appointment to meet with her. I've already instructed her to make this the wedding of your dreams."

Haley couldn't believe he was willing to do that for her. "But why, Luke?"

"You deserve so much better than our first wedding, sweetheart. I want everyone we know to be at this ceremony and see how special you are to me and how honored I am that you're my wife." He brushed a strand of hair from her cheek and his tender touch sent tingling sensations down her body. "And this time around, there aren't going to be any business meetings or labor disputes to keep me from being with you every second of our wedding day and night."

"I love you," she whispered, tears streaming down both cheeks.

"And I love you," he proclaimed, placing the other piece of paper in her hand. "This is the address and phone number of Millie Sanford."

"My...mother?" she reiterated, staring at the small note. "But how did you find her? I don't even remember telling you her name."

"Let's just say I know a woman with a hell of an investigative team and leave it at that," he said, giving her a smile that melted her heart. "You may or may not want to use that information, but I wanted you to have it in case you decide to get in touch with her."

Unable to stop the tears from rolling down her cheeks, she wrapped her arms around his shoulders and hugged him close as she sobbed against his shoulder. "I love you so much, Luke Garnier," she rasped when she finally managed to bring her emotions back under control. "Thank you."

He placed his hand on her stomach and when he met her gaze, the love she detected in his eyes sent delightful shivers up her spine. "By the way, I think you might want to consider reducing your hours at the office now that you're pregnant."

"Why?"

"Because if you're working all day, I can't pamper you the way you deserve," he informed, kissing her forehead.

Laying her head on his shoulder, she sighed. "I've never been pampered before in my entire life."

"I know and as your husband, I intend to remedy that problem." His tone left no doubt that that was exactly what he would do.

Placing her hand over his still resting on her stomach, she grinned. "I was thinking that I might even quit."

"Or you could work from home. That is if you think you'll get anything done with me and the baby under-foot all day?"

"What do you mean?"

"I'm going to start working from home in order to be with you through your pregnancy and help out with the baby once he's born," he announced, smiling.

Happier than she'd ever been in her life, Haley laughed. "Ever since you asked me to have a baby, you've referred to it as 'he' or your 'son.' What if we have a little girl?"

"You've mentioned that before and I've given it some thought," he said, his smile filled with love. "A little girl as sweet and wonderful as her mother would be just fine with me. We can have two or three boys a few years down the line."

She gave him a mock frown. "Two or three?"

Resting his forehead against her, he winked. "Sweet-heart, I love you so much I'll be more than willing to give you all the babies you want. Girls, boys, twins, whatever your heart desires."

"Really?" Nothing would thrill her more than having a whole houseful of Garnier children to mother.

"I love you, Haley Garnier. More than you'll ever know."

"And I love you, Luke. With all of my heart and soul."

Epilogue

After receiving good-natured advice from Caleb, Nick and Hunter, Luke smiled at Jake. "Looks like the next brother to take the plunge will be you."

Jake snorted. "If I were you, I wouldn't hold my breath. You'd end up turning blue and passing out before I take a trip down the aisle."

"Never say 'never,'" Hunter said, laughing. "It'll come back to bite you in the butt every time."

"Gentlemen, it's time to take your places," the wedding coordinator reported, motioning for them to follow the minister.

Walking to the front of the ballroom, Luke couldn't wait to see Haley. Arielle and his half brothers' wives had rented a suite at the hotel and insisted on Haley spending the night before the wedding with them. And even though he and his brothers had a great time hanging out at his house, Luke had missed being with her, holding her all through the night and waking up with her in his arms that morning.

When the double doors opened at the back of the room and the bridesmaids came down the aisle to take their places on the opposite side of the minister, his breath stalled and Luke couldn't believe how stunning Haley looked as she stepped onto the satin runner. She'd been beautiful the day they'd exchanged vows in the little chapel in the mountains, but today she was absolutely radiant.

Luke stepped forward to extend his arm and when she smiled up at him with more love than he deserved, he silently vowed to spend the rest of his life making sure she never doubted how much he loved her in return. "Are you ready to renew your vows to be my wife?"

"As ready as I am to hear your vows to be my husband," she noted, her sweet voice sending a shaft of heat straight through him.

"I love you, today, tomorrow and for the rest of our lives, sweetheart."

"And I will always love you," she promised, making him feel like the luckiest man alive.

"Isn't this just wonderful, Luther?" Emerald asked, leaning over to her personal assistant when the bride and groom turned to face the minister. "Four of my grandchildren married in a little over three years."

Luther gave her his usual stiff nod. "I'd say you've outdone yourself, Mrs. Larson."

Yes, everything had come together just as she'd

planned. With information supplied by her good friend and curator at the museum, Max Parmelli, her arrangement to hire Chet Parker for the entertainment at her reception she'd thrown for herself last month had worked out brilliantly. The young singer's interest in the lovely Haley had been just the impetus Luke needed to help him realize his feelings for her and ultimately led to Emerald watching them renew their vows.

She smiled as she gazed at the wedding party standing at the front of the Opryland Hotel's main ballroom. Luke made such a handsome groom and she'd never seen him look happier. Jake, the best man, was the mirror image of the groom and she still marveled at how much they resembled their father, Owen. She dabbed a tear that slipped from her eye with an Irish linen handkerchief. If only Owen could have realized what a precious gift his children were.

Her gaze drifted to her three other grandsons, Caleb, Nick and Hunter, and her heart swelled with emotion. It thrilled her to know that Luke and Jake had become close to their newfound brothers. And she was doubly happy that Luke had asked them to be groomsmen in his and Haley's wedding.

She sighed contentedly. Now that everything had worked out for Luke, she could turn her attention to making sure the same happened for her remaining unmarried grandchildren.

She focused her attention on Jake. He was going to be the most challenging one yet. Of all of her grandchildren, she worried that he might be the one who turned out to be just like his father. And although she'd yet to determine the best course of action to test his mettle, she had already started collecting information and she had no doubt that something would come to mind for him very soon.

Turning her attention to her only granddaughter Arielle, Emerald smiled fondly. With a baby on the way and her mother Francesca gone, the child needed Emerald now more than ever. But she had already set the wheels in motion to remedy the situation and she had every confidence that it would be brought to a satisfying conclusion, the same as her other efforts for all of her grandchildren.

"Aren't they a beautiful couple?" she queried Luther when Luke and Haley turned to walk back up the aisle as the string quartet played Pachelbel's Canon.

"A handsome couple indeed," Luther agreed, nodding.

Emerald smiled beatifically. "That's another one down."

Luther came as close to smiling as he was capable of doing. "And two more to go, madam."

* * * * *

Don't miss Kathie DeNosky's next
THE ILLEGITIMATE HEIRS *release,*
ONE NIGHT, TWO BABIES
On sale September 8, 2009
from Silhouette Desire.

RICK'S APPOINTMENT with his attorney early Wednesday morning went only moderately better than his meeting with social services the day before. The prognosis wasn't great—but at least his attorney was going to file a motion for DNA testing. Just so Rick could petition to see the child…his sister's baby. The sister he didn't know he had until it was too late.

The rest of what his attorney said had been downhill from there.

Cell phone in hand before he'd even reached his Nitro, Rick punched in the speed dial number he'd programmed the day before.

Maybe foster parent Sue Bookman hadn't received his message. Or had lost his number. Maybe she didn't want to talk to him. At this point he didn't much care what she wanted.

"Hello?" She answered before the first ring was complete. And sounded breathless.

Young and breathless.

"Ms. Bookman?"

"Yes. This is Rick Kraynick, right?"

"Yes, ma'am."

"I recognized your number on caller ID," she said, her voice uneven, as though she was still engaged in whatever physical activity had her so breathless to begin with. "I'm sorry I didn't get back to you. I've been a little...distracted."

The words came in more disjointed spurts. Was she jogging?

"No problem," he said, when, in fact, he'd spent the better part of the night before watching his phone. And fretting. "Did I get you at a bad time?"

"No worse than usual," she said, adding, "Better than some. So, how can I help?"

God, if only this could be so easy. He'd ask. She'd help. And life could go well. At least for one little person in his family.

It would be a first.

"Mr. Kraynick?"

"Yes. Sorry. I was...are you sure there isn't a better time to call?"

"I'm bouncing a baby, Mr. Kraynick. It's what I do."

"Is it Carrie?" he asked quickly, his pulse racing.

"How do you know Carrie?" She sounded defensive, which wouldn't do him any good.

"I'm her uncle," he explained, "her mother's—Christy's—older brother, and I know you have her."

"I can neither confirm nor deny your allegations, Mr. Kraynick. Please call social services." She rattled off the number.

"Wait!" he said, unable to hide his urgency. "Please," he said more calmly. "Just hear me out."

"How did you find me?"

"A friend of Christy's."

"I'm sorry I can't help you, Mr. Kraynick," she said softly. "This conversation is over."

"I grew up in foster care," he said, as though that gave him some special privilege. Some insider's edge.

"Then you know you shouldn't be calling me at all."

"Yes… But Carrie is my niece," he said. "I need to see her. To know that she's okay."

"You'll have to go through social services to arrange that."

"I'm sure you know it's not as easy as it sounds. I'm a single man with no real ties and I've no intention of petitioning for custody. They aren't real eager to give me the time of day. I never even knew Carrie's mother. For all intents and purposes, our mother didn't raise either one of us. All I have going for me is half a set of genes. My lawyer's on it, but it could be weeks— months—before this is sorted out. Carrie could be adopted by then. Which would be fine, great for her, but then I'd have lost my chance. I don't want to take her. I won't hurt her. I just have to see her."

"I'm sorry, Mr. Kraynick, but…"

* * * * *

*Find out if Rick Kraynick will ever have
a chance to meet his niece.
Look for A DAUGHTER'S TRUST
by Tara Taylor Quinn,
available in September 2009.*